Rafael called her name in a low whisper and as she looked up at him, he cupped the nape of her neck with his hand, tangled his fingers into her short, dark hair—and kissed her.

That kiss.

The last thing Sammy had been expecting. The mouth that covered hers was cool, and devastatingly powerful. She was so surprised that she didn't pull back, so stunned that she lost herself in it and yielded to a drowning sensation quite unlike anything she had ever felt in her life before.

She tiptoed to return the kiss. Her hand crept along his neck and curved the shape of his jaw just as he pulled away and murmured, with husky amusement, "Thank you."

In a heartbeat, she realized what had just happened. About to introduce the love of his life to his guests and fearing that *love* was probably the last thing on her face, he had pulled her to him and kissed her, kissed her until she was soft and compliant and rosy cheeked, *kissed her senseless.*

Cathy Williams can remember reading Harlequin books as a teenager, and now that she is writing them, she remains an avid fan. For her, there is nothing like creating romantic stories and engaging plots, and each and every book is a new adventure. Cathy lives in London, and her three daughters—Charlotte, Olivia and Emma—have always been, and continue to be, the greatest inspirations in her life.

Books by Cathy Williams

Harlequin Presents

Desert King's Surprise Love-Child
Consequences of Their Wedding Charade
Hired by the Forbidden Italian
Bound by a Nine-Month Confession
A Week with the Forbidden Greek
The Housekeeper's Invitation to Italy
The Italian's Innocent Cinderella
Unveiled as the Italian's Bride
Bound by Her Baby Revelation

Secrets of Billionaires' Secretaries

A Wedding Negotiation with Her Boss
Royally Promoted

Visit the Author Profile page
at Harlequin.com for more titles.

EMERGENCY ENGAGEMENT

CATHY WILLIAMS

Harlequin

PRESENTS

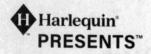 **Harlequin®**
PRESENTS™

ISBN-13: 978-1-335-93921-0

Emergency Engagement

Copyright © 2024 by Cathy Williams

Recycling programs for this product may not exist in your area.

 Harlequin Enterprises ULC
22 Adelaide St. West, 41st Floor
Toronto, Ontario M5H 4E3, Canada
www.Harlequin.com

Printed in Lithuania

MIX
Paper | Supporting responsible forestry
FSC® C021394

EMERGENCY
ENGAGEMENT

To my wonderful daughter Emma and the inspiration that she is.

CHAPTER ONE

AND...BREATHE... You'RE here now, so just...breathe.

Unlike the brash glass towers everywhere, the Moreno HQ was housed in an anonymous grey, five-storey, brutalist slab that felt threatening in its lack of pretentiousness. Inside, however, was an eye-watering marvel of pale marble, glass and concrete. Sammy, head down and walking at speed towards the reception area, cut a slight and unimposing figure: five-foot-three, close-cropped dark hair with skin as pale as milk and huge, cut-glass green eyes. Under one arm was her portfolio: five years of hopes, dreams and ambitions were contained within, not to mention blood, sweat and tears.

Most businesses in the heart of London would have been bustling with people. At least, that was what Sammy had vaguely assumed. Here, however, it was an oasis of deathly calm—very unnerving, to say the least. She wished that she'd made a stand and insisted on Rafael Moreno travelling to Yorkshire to see *her,* instead of her having to make her way to London, at great personal expense. He was the one who was in the process of ruining her life, after all.

Fat chance of that happening, though.

Phil, the assistant bank manager at the local building society, had been brilliant over the months and years with all her financial stuff. She had gone to school with him, and had been in his class right the way through, and he had suggested to Clifford that he could do her a favour and get her a meeting with Rafael. It was the way it worked in a small place where everyone knew everyone else.

So travelling to London? It was a small price to pay to see the Big Man, Sammy thought without an ounce of gratitude.

She padded her way to the ice-cold, smoothly polished concrete desk behind which two incredibly beautiful girls sat in front of a bank of wafer-thin laptops.

'I have an appointment with Mr Moreno.'

'Name, please?'

'Samantha Payne.' She waited while an impeccably groomed blonde took a rudely long time scrolling through her screen before nodding, without bothering to look at her at all.

'You can go up—top floor. You'll be met there. I've been advised to tell you that Mr Moreno works to a tight schedule. He can't spare you more than half an hour.'

'I'll make sure to be grateful for small mercies,' Sammy muttered under her breath, turning towards the small bank of discreet chrome lifts that blended seamlessly into the pale-grey walls.

Her heart was pounding as the lift purred its way up four floors. She could have taken the stairs—she would have welcomed the exercise as a little extra thinking time—but the business of asking where they were seemed more trouble than it was worth. Besides, there was such a thing as too much thinking time. Too much thinking time risked teetering into unhelpful panic.

Rafael Moreno: the self-made billionaire whose face seemed to be relentlessly plastered on the cover of every tabloid gossip magazine month after month, although he was so much more than just a sexy guy with an army of women swooning over him. He was also the golden boy who had made a fortune before he'd turned twenty-five—a tech genius who had refused to be limited to just tech and had moved some of his considerable fortune into other, equally profitable areas that included commercial developments, boutique hotels across the world and, most recently, his own wine label.

He was the guy who couldn't be stopped when it came to climbing the ladder. In fact, Sammy reckoned that, when it came to Rafael Moreno, there were no more rungs left. He'd climbed all of them and was aiming for whatever there was beyond ladders.

Crazy, when she looked back and remembered the boy he used to be. She didn't think Rafael Moreno did much looking back, though, but who knew?

Suddenly, the lift doors opened and, sure enough, there was another stunning woman waiting to escort her through to wherever Rafael had his office.

Here, at least, there was the quiet hum of vast sums of money being made. Sammy had no idea who occupied the other floors of the building but the men and women here, all decked out in snappy clothes, were serious and focused, and barely glanced in her direction as she walked by the open space with its clever glass partitions and luscious plants. How many screens did one person need, anyway? Everyone seemed to be facing an army of them on their chrome-and-glass desks. There were more computers here than people.

'I should advise you that Mr Moreno…'

'Yes.' Sammy pre-empted what was coming. 'Is a very busy man who only has half an hour to spare for me. I was already warned by the girl downstairs. Don't worry, I don't plan on locking the door and keeping him prisoner until he hears what I have to say.'

This was met with stony silence that lasted until an imposing door was pushed open…and then, on the threshold of his office, nerves really kicked in. Yes, she'd seen his picture here and there in grainy print; and yes, she'd often glanced at reports of his meteoric progress in the financial jungle, where he took no prisoners; but was she ready to meet this guy? Maybe not…

She disapproved of him on every level. She'd disapproved of him fifteen years ago when he'd entered their small, comfortably cushioned world in the back of beyond like something from another planet, disrupting routines and flouting conventions. And she disapproved of him now because, from every report she'd ever seen, he'd become just what she'd expected—a guy who played by his own rules and didn't give a damn about anybody else. A man who didn't glance over his shoulder to see what havoc he might have left in his wake.

He had his back to her and was staring out of the window but then he turned round slowly, giving her plenty of time to realise that he was still as sinfully sexy as he had been as a sixteen-year-old—with his raven-black hair, dark, dark eyes with eyelashes any girl would kill for, his features chiselled to perfection.

The only difference was this was no boy. This was a man: tougher, harder, colder...the sharp contours of his face betraying experiences learned over the years in a ruthless climb to the top.

She'd wondered whether he would recognise her. Fifteen years was a long time; she'd been a kid of just twelve, invisible behind her shyness and early adolescence.

He didn't have a clue who she was. She could see it in his cool, closed expression as he looked at her in silence for a few seconds.

'Sit.'

Noticeably, he remained lounging by the window as she shuffled to the chair in front of his desk and rested her portfolio on the ground next to her.

'You're here about the hotel.'

Rafael strolled towards his desk, dark eyes pinned to the elfin girl in front of him whose face looked vaguely familiar, although he was damned if he could put his finger on it.

He knew what she was here about: some nonsense about the hotel he had bought. Of course, the deed was done; the hotel up in Yorkshire, along with the various outbuildings on either side of it, belonged to him. He had bought the lot and he had no intention of yielding to any bleeding-heart sob stories about slicing up his acquisition to share with anyone else.

But he had some experience of people from that part of the world. It was a closed community, suspicious of outsiders and happy to close ranks to make life difficult for them. He didn't fancy a difficult life, so he'd agreed to this meeting—but it was going to be a waste of time for both of them.

He glanced at his watch and, when he looked back at her, her eyes were cool and scornful. They were green eyes, clear as glass, framed by thick, dark lashes and set against smooth, pale skin. Under the heavy jumper and thick, dark skirt, which he suspected had been worn in a token gesture to the fact that this was a meeting of sorts, she was slight. Her dark hair was very short, but it suited her, emphasising the delicacy of her heart-shaped face and the hugeness of those green eyes.

Right now, however, there was nothing fragile about either her posture or her expression.

'I'm here about the outbuilding attached to the hotel, to be precise.'

'This is hardly orthodox,' Rafael drawled, moving to sit behind the desk so that she now felt in the position of someone being interviewed for a job she wasn't going to get. 'Cutting to the chase, I've bought the hotel, just as I've bought the places alongside it. As you'll probably know, I have every intention of developing the lot into a niche boutique hotel, and taking those acres of tumbleweed and overgrown fields and doing something creative with them. A mower might prove to be a good start on that. I've cast an eye over your objections and it would seem that…' he scrolled through his computer, then looked at her '…your plans were to buy one of the outbuildings for yourself?'

'Correct.'

'That's unfortunate for you. You have my heartfelt sympathy but business, as you know, is business.'

'This is more than just *about business* for me,' Sammy said through gritted teeth. 'I've spent *years* putting money aside so that I can accumulate a deposit to buy somewhere suitable for my venture. That outbuilding was my dream come true because I had also got someone in to look at converting the upstairs into a place for me to live.'

'And that's a shame,' Rafael said politely. 'You might have something to say about Clifford selling the hotel to me, when he'd presumably already accepted an offer from you for the building attached to it, but…' He shrugged—as if, "what do you expect me to do?"—and kept his eyes pinned to her face.

'I have, as it happens! You offered him a stupid amount of money. His daughter is ill and that sort of money would mean that he'd be able to give her private medical treatment. He was in a no-win position.'

'Hardly my fault.'

'The hotel was doing fine, Mr Moreno! It was making sufficient money with the regulars, and in the summer months it was holding its own. It's part of the community. It's been there for over eighty years—and you want to bulldoze it!'

'It's decrepit and in need of some serious money spending on it. Plus, it's heading in the wrong direction when it comes to making a profit. Trust me on this, Miss Payne. This is my business—I can spot something living on borrowed time from a mile away. There was no way Clifford was going to be able to keep on top of the repairs. He knew that. I did him a favour. If your little concern happened to fall by the wayside, then you need to step back and look at the bigger picture.'

'The bigger picture being the usual situation of a large, faceless conglomerate consuming the small, family business? Clifford and I had agreed that the money he made from selling that side-building to me would have gone towards upgrading the hotel!'

'I know how much he offered you the place for. It would have been a drop in the ocean when it comes to making a dent in the work needed to haul that decaying old place into the twenty-first century.'

Sammy swallowed and tried to control her temper which was threatening to break its leash and run haywire. She dropped her eyes and clasped her fingers on her lap.

'Why did you come here?' Rafael asked softly. 'Was it to try and get me to change my mind—even though the machinery has already started rolling for completion on the new hotel within the next couple of weeks?'

'I've worked my fingers to the bone for the past five years.' She did her best not to sound self-pitying, because by the looks of it this wasn't a guy who empathised with anyone's plight. 'Worked to get myself into a place where I could actually buy somewhere to open my patisserie and café. I've sorted out all the equipment and it hasn't been cheap. I've done the maths and worked out how to make a living doing what I love and what I'm good at. Clifford felt awful about selling to you. I was the first person he told. He suggested...'

'What did he suggest?'

'He suggested that you sell the outbuilding to me. If you want to somehow modernise it to fit in with your plans for the hotel, then maybe we could work out a re-payment plan. I know it'll make money—with its location, and it being attached to the hotel, there's footfall. I would be willing to pay the mortgage even if I couldn't set up business immediately, even if I had to wait for work to be done...'

Rafael burst out laughing.

'My apologies,' he said, without a trace of apology in his voice. 'But let me show you something.'

He fiddled on the keyboard and then swivelled the screen round so that she was looking at it, then he vaulted upright, his body long, lean and fluid, and swerved to stand behind her. He leant down, his hand resting on the arm of the leather chair in which she was sitting, and pointed to the screen.

Sammy's vision blurred. She could make out something impressive and fancy, spinning round on the screen to afford a view from several angles, but it was hard to focus on anything because every nerve in her body was quivering at his sudden proximity.

'So, you understand why that would be impossible?'

'Sorry?'

Rafael stood up and then perched on the edge of his desk so that now she had nowhere to look but at him… and the the brown column of his neck where the white shirt was unbuttoned, cuffed to the elbows, the way the dark whorls of hair curled around the metal strap of his watch and the tight pull of his trousers over muscular thighs. Memories of her fourteen-year-old self gazing at him from the side-lines in those long summer months before he and his father had upped sticks and left now accosted her, making her thinking sluggish and woolly.

'Clifford owned a hotel rooted in the past,' Rafael said. He was talking slowly and gently, the voice of someone trying to explain the obvious to a halfwit. 'The entire lay-out of the place left a lot to be desired. Some of the bed-rooms actually shared a bathroom! Others had fireplaces that were so blocked, it's a wonder they weren't a regis-tered fire hazard. It might have been languishing in its faded glory as a traditional timepiece, ticking along like an ancient grandfather clock, but that formula no longer works in this day and age. Those outbuildings? Falling apart at the seams. Destined for landfill, I'm afraid. The beautiful countryside in that part of the world demands something that people actually want to pay money to stay in, and that hotel and everything alongside it stopped fit-ting the bill fifty years ago.'

'Clifford's great-grandfather…'

'Look, don't get me wrong, I sympathise with you and I admire you for having the guts to come here and make your case. But the truth is, I'm doing you a favour. If you'd bought that outbuilding, you would have found yourself lumbered with a liability in five years' time when the main hotel started to fall apart.'

Rafael swept aside any further pointless objections with a wave of his hand. 'As a gesture of goodwill, I will reimburse you for any money you might have spent in the expectation of getting the place, although I'm assuming you will be able to make use of whatever equipment you may have bought wherever you end up?'

He paused, allowing an uncomfortable silence to gather between them before continuing with an elegant shrug, 'I'll admit that the prospect of a patisserie would have held considerable appeal, especially with the up-stairs done up as a place of residence, but I have no inten-tion of keeping that building. It would require too much work, given the state that it's in, and besides, there's no place for it, as you've seen for yourself from what I've just shown you. My team of architects lean more towards a minimalist look than shambolic clutter.'

He stood up, looked down at her for a few seconds and frowned.

'Do I know you from somewhere?'

Sammy gazed back at him with a sinking heart.

'So, there's nothing I can do to persuade you to…?'

'Completely reconfigure the design of the hotel so that I can incorporate your plans through sheer good-ness of heart? No. I'm afraid not. And, like I said…' his voice grew more gentle '…you're better off finding some-where that wouldn't end up on the scrap heap anyway in a few years' time. Surely there are other premises you could look at?'

'My heart was set on Rafter's Hotel. Like I said, it's a really important part of the community, and it fitted the bill in so many ways. I'm sure whatever problems there were with the building's age could have been handled.' She raised her eyes to look him directly in the eye. 'If you had no intention of doing anything about the situation, why did you bother seeing me in the first place?'

'Good question, and deserving of an answer. Truth is, I like to do my due diligence when it comes to my hotels.'

'Your due diligence?'

'Make sure I'm not going to be treading on anyone's toes. You'd be surprised how tedious it can be dealing with a cohort of people who decide to make a stand against something they don't want.'

'And the general consensus was…?'

'That a renovation would do a lot to revive the community. My hotels come with a solid reputation and the year-round tourist influx would benefit a host of small businesses. Naturally, if Clifford had chosen not to sell, I would have shrugged and moved on, but I managed to make him see sense. I can assure you that I was extremely generous in my offer. He got a hell of a lot more from me than he would have from anyone else. Aside from that, I agreed to meet with you because, like I said, you deserved to be told first-hand why your deal went belly-up. I may be a businessman but I'm not without some sympathy for what you're going through.'

'You over-paid for the hotel?'

'I'm a generous guy.'

'I didn't realise billionaires made their money by feeling sorry for people.'

'I have a personal tie to that part of the world, if you really want to know.'

'Royal Stanton Grammar.'

She knew the school he'd attended for the two years he'd been living in the village adjacent to the one in which the hotel was located. Their eyes met and he held her gaze as he rooted through his memories, trying to dredge up any recollection of her.

His dark eyes narrowed and she fidgeted.

'So I *do* know you...'

'You were in Stanton for two years,' Sammy confirmed.

'So I was. I don't recall your name...'

'It was a long time ago and you've turned into a billionaire since then. No surprise you haven't got a clue who I am. Making billions must have taken quite a bit of your time.'

'Payne... Payne...' he said softly, frowning. He sat back and stared out through the window before looking at her once again. 'Did you plan on using your familiarity with me to your advantage?'

'No. I hadn't planned on telling you that I knew who you were at all.'

'Samantha Payne.' His eyes stayed fixed on her pale face and he tilted his head to one side and stared. Of course, he recognised her now, and was surprised he

hadn't sooner—but then he hadn't been expecting someone from his past to show up in his present.

He'd been truthful when he'd told her he'd wanted to
do the decent thing and explain the situation first-hand—
while still, of course, making sure to impress on her that
he was intransigent in his decision. Now, he felt a reluctant admiration for her tenacity in not backing down,
even though she must have remembered that, well, even
as a teenager, backing down had never been his thing.

'I should go.'

Rafael didn't say anything. He wasn't about to embark
on a voyage down memory lane. Yet, against his better
judgement, he remembered those strange, unsettling days
when he and his father had gone to the very village she
had mentioned because his father had managed to land
himself a two-year stint working on a building site eight
miles away. It had been a basic job but anything had been
better than staying put in the East End of London with
his father buried in misery and depression because he'd
found that his wife hadn't just been unfaithful once, or
twice, but too many times to count…

Theirs had been a volatile, disintegrating marriage to
which his father had desperately clung even when the
arguments had come on a daily basis—a marriage that
should never have happened. It had been washed up in
a series of confessions that Isabella Moreno hadn't bothered to hide from her only son, sixteen years old and
growing harder and tougher with each shouted, gloat-
ing, embittered revelation. Yes, he had loved his father,

but he had also pitied him for not having the strength to walk away from what had been bad for him.

Accusations had been hurled and tears had been shed. If Rafael hadn't grown up by then, he'd certainly grown up afterwards, when the dust had settled and his mother had left arm in arm with her new, rich lover and no forwarding address.

'You're a big boy now,' had been her parting words to Rafael. 'You don't need me here any longer.'

'Did I ever?' he had returned, before leaving the house for a welcome dose of fresh air.

His father had lost the plot. At the time, Rafael had had no idea why. It wasn't as though theirs had ever been a marriage made in heaven. To a child, it had been black and white: it was teenage lust that had propelled his parents into an unwanted pregnancy. Juan Miguel Moreno, aged just eighteen, had walked a very pregnant Isabella Gutierrez up the aisle, she too only just eighteen, only for her to give birth a fortnight later.

From memory, things hadn't been bad to start with, but time had put paid to any notion of their marriage working. Rafael had grown up knowing just how frustrated his mother felt at being with a guy who adored her but was never going to make enough money to keep her satisfied.

She'd been the opposite of a domestic goddess. She'd worked shifts, although afterwards Rafael reckoned she'd been doing a whole lot more than working. She'd gone out without saying where to, and she'd left her husband to pick up the slack on the home front.

Why she hadn't left sooner was a mystery—perhaps the habit of her marriage and the predictability of a husband she no longer loved but still relied upon had kept her rooted until someone rich had come along to rescue her. After she'd left, his father had taken to the bottle to cope. If the job offer many miles away in some nice, healthy countryside hadn't come along, Lord only knew where things would have ended up. But they had gone to that little village with its little village school and...

'Colin Payne.' He looked at the elfin figure in front of him with her defiance and her angry green eyes and made the connection.

Before she could say anything, his intercom buzzed and his PA reminded him of the meeting he had at the Shard.

Without taking his eyes from her face, Rafael told his PA that he wouldn't make it and, before she could recover from her astonishment, he surprised her further by telling her to cancel whatever remained on his calendar for the rest of the day.

'I thought you could only spare me half an hour,' Sammy said coolly.

'Things change.'

'Nothing's changed. You can't or won't do anything to help me, and I get it. It was stupid of me to think otherwise.'

'Colin Payne was your brother. *Is* your brother.'

Sammy shrugged.

'He was in my form for the two years we were at school together,' Rafael recalled.

'I didn't realise that you were ever *at* school. I thought school was just somewhere you visited now and again when it took your fancy.'

'Good times, bad times,' he murmured with a sudden grin. 'I admit, I didn't set a good example when it came to behaviour back in those days.'

'Actually, that's the understatement of the decade. But that was a long time ago and I haven't come here to reminisce.'

'I remember your brother and…now that I think about it… I remember *you*. You were very shy, always peeping from under that fringe of yours. Your hair was long back then—probably why I didn't recognise you immediately. I have a keen eye for faces.'

'Like I said, Mr Moreno, I didn't come here to talk about the past.'

Rafael watched the rise of delicate colour in her cheeks, shaken out of his usual steely self-control and aware of her—not just as someone to whom he conceded he owed an explanation, but as someone who…belonged to memories he had put away in a box, hidden and never to be aired. He was surprised that he hadn't remembered sooner because she did, in fact, have quite a distinctive face. Those eyes…

'You must have been…what…thirteen, fourteen when I had called it a day with A Levels and was packing my bags to leave? You weren't like the other girls, that's for sure.'

'You mean the other girls who kept begging for your attention?'

'Adolescence can be a heady time for some.'

'Not you, though. You ignored all of them. You missed the backstage tears.'

'I was more fascinated by the older women back then.'

'Good to know. Thank you for your time.'

She began to gather her things to leave, but Rafael stopped her by asking, 'What's your brother doing now? He wanted to go into medicine, if I remember.'

'He's a nurse now. He ended up having to repeat a year after you disappeared. He'd always been a model student until you came along.'

Rafael didn't say anything. He remembered what life had been like back then, with his father a mess and him having to pick up the pieces. Rafael had had to make sure he got himself off to work and not back on the bottle because they'd needed the money to survive. He remembered himself as an angry, disillusioned, confused teenaged boy raging against the world, loving his fragile father but hating him at the same time.

There had been a lot of truancy back then but he'd been so bright that he'd never fallen behind. He hadn't asked anyone to copy him, but some of the other boys in his class had followed his lead. He'd been too wrapped up in his own anger to give much of a damn about how skipping classes might affect them.

That said, he wasn't in the business of apologising to anyone for anything. Besides, tough times made for tough people, and tough people did well in life. They knew how to handle its obstacles. He was a fine example of that.

'I never encouraged anyone to follow me.'

'But you never did anything to discourage them, either!'

'I did my own thing. I wasn't in the business of setting examples to anyone. At the time, there were more interesting things to do than listening to teachers who really didn't know as much as me and, if there were kids who wanted to fall in with that, then who was I to start preaching to them?'

'That's incredibly arrogant!'

'Maybe, or maybe I'm just being honest. I'm sorry if you feel that your brother went off the rails because of me, although it's probably healthier to think that everyone is responsible for the decisions they make. It's counter-productive to blame other people for their own poor choices. Send him my regards and, like I said, I would be happy to compensate you for any loss on whatever equipment you may have bought. I mean that. It took guts coming here and I admire you for that.'

She was already rising to her feet and heading to the door. He didn't try to stop her. He wasn't going to change his plans just because they happened to share a tenuous connection.

But he had to force himself not to follow her. Instead, he remained where he was, watching the angry sway of her slender hips as she stormed out of the door.

Lord only knew what his PA in the adjoining office made of the fuming slip of a thing who had just slammed a door behind her. Generally speaking, no one slammed doors behind them when they left his office, not even ex-girlfriends, which was a good thing; there had been enough angry exes to make the building rattle if they ever decided to join forces and slam doors.

Rafael enjoyed a colourful love life. He enjoyed women and, when he was dating, he was one hundred percent attentive and faithful. He just wasn't into staying the course. He didn't have the appetite for the disillusioning business of marriage and the pointless hope that fuelled it. He was always honest about that—some might say to a fault—but still, many an angry ex who had expected the unattainable would have slammed doors had they not feared his disapproval.

This woman, though… She hadn't thought twice. He rose to his feet, suddenly edgy. When he glanced down, it was to find that she had forgotten the folder she had brought with her and dumped on the ground by the chair.

It was too late to chase her down the road waving a folder…not his style anyway. He would have a look to see if a contact number was anywhere inside, or at the very least her email address. He would get his PA to do the honours and return it.

He settled into his leather chair, kept all calls on hold and flipped open the portfolio she had managed to forget in her furious haste.

Halfway to Harrogate on the train, Sammy belatedly remembered the damned portfolio. It had taken her days to meticulously prepare her business plan, but no way was she going to turn around and go back for it. Nor was she going to phone and ask for it to be sent.

Frankly, after the reception she'd been given, it was

probably winging its way to the dump by now. She hadn't given it a passing thought because she'd been so worked up when she'd stormed out of his office, slamming the door behind her, aware of his glamorous PA half-rising to her feet in shock as she'd swept by. All those uninterested people who hadn't noticed when she'd arrived had sat up and taken stock when she'd left—which had almost made her smile, except the last thing she'd been in the mood to do had been to crack a smile at anything.

Of course, it was the mention of her brother that had been her undoing. She had been shocked that he'd recognised her and then to remember Colin…and, to top it off, to remember her as the shy thing peeping at him while all the bolder girls had flaunted themselves in the smallest outfits they could get away with.

She stared through the window at scenery flashing past.

Rafael and Colin had been in the same form. Who could ever have predicted that Colin, always so quiet and studious, would have become a dedicated member of Rafael's fan club? He'd gone off the rails, in true Rafael Moreno style and had dumped the school books for skipping class, as if he'd been making up for all that lost time when he'd been so diligent. Then, Rafael had disappeared in a puff of smoke, and her brother had discovered how woefully behind he had fallen. He'd failed four of the eight exams he'd taken. Rafael Moreno might have been capable of attending one class and still getting straight As, but no one else had been, including her brother. Everything had been delayed a year and her mother, fragile after the divorce, had become a bag of nerves all over again.

Sammy simmered and fumed and wondered what the hell happened now. She would have to start looking into things in the coming week. She rented somewhere at the moment, but she'd blithely given in her notice because she'd anticipated the fun of living above her café and doing the place up, somewhere that would be all hers. The thought of getting back in the rental market yet again made her feel sick. Her mum lived ten miles away in the nearest town. Should she migrate there for a while?

Sammy knew that she should feel angry and betrayed, because she had set her hopes high, had had it all just within her grasp... But how on earth could she be angry with Clifford when concerns for his ill daughter had driven his decision?

It was quite a lot to think about and yet, with all those pressing worries on her mind, she found herself drifting off to sleep, thinking of something else of a very different nature.

Or rather, *someone* else.

Rafael, with his darkly forbidding good looks and eyes that seemed to bore straight into her. He'd looked at her and she'd felt herself go hot and cold and then hot all over again. All she could hope was that he hadn't noticed.

He'd made her relive a youthful infatuation and she hated that. She might not have openly flung herself into his path like some of the other girls but, as twelve had turned to fourteen, she had done her fair share of daydreaming. She'd been no different from everyone else.

Like them, she had never met anyone as fascinating or as good-looking as Rafael Moreno.

She'd been smart enough not to show it, but it seemed that he'd noticed her looking from the side-lines anyway: a thin, boyish, self-conscious adolescent without any of the generous assets all the other girls had seemed to have.

Memories floated in and out as she fell asleep, and they didn't have the decency to leave her alone even then; when the train pulled into the station, she woke to realise that she'd been dreaming of the damned man.

CHAPTER TWO

RAFAEL LOOKED AT Sammy's unprepossessing house from behind the wheel of his sleek, black BMW. The house was nestled in a row of similarly plain houses and was a pointed reminder of what he had escaped. The claustrophobia which had engulfed him for the two years he and his father had put down roots in a town very close to this one swirled around him. There was so much love for and impatience with his dad wrapped up in a small village where everybody knew everybody else—not to mention hope and despair.

He knew that this was a sweeping and unfair judgement of the place, but it was one that came from his gut. He had paid a fleeting visit back to the area when he had decided to build his hotel because, aside from his own personal experiences, the place was one of tremendous natural beauty, more than capable of holding its own against the saturated Cotswolds countryside or Cornish coastline, and it was ripe for just the sort of development he had in mind. If this worked out, he would consider something commercial in the area. It would be perfect for the sort of business development that wasn't reliant on access to London and he had a number of companies that would thrive in the wild Yorkshire Dales.

Coming here now felt more personal because he was back to see someone who had been a part of his life all those years ago. She'd lodged in his head since she'd showed up at this office the day before. He'd pictured her fierce, determined face, relived the shock of seeing her in the first place and had known that, thanks to her, a Pandora's box of memories had been opened that he hadn't been able to squash since she'd stormed out. He wasn't the sort who had much time for a past that couldn't be changed, but it seemed that the past didn't have much respect for that, and had decided to reassert itself after over a decade of conveniently hibernating.

Rafael could have simply posted the portfolio back to her, or emailed her to arrange a drop-off, but in the end he had decided on the spur of the moment to hand-deliver it. He could use the opportunity to visit the land agent and have another look around the hotel and the properties so that he could determine what he wanted to do before delegating his instructions.

He'd debated whether to phone ahead first, but in the end had decided to simply swing by. The fact that the first page of her portfolio was generous with information about where she lived and the various ways in which she could be contacted seemed to be fate inviting him to pay her visit.

And, in truth, reading through the pack she had prepared for him had opened his eyes to a guilty conscience he hadn't thought he possessed: guilt that he could have been more sympathetic to his father; guilt that his antics must have meant yet more worries for him at the time. He had since set up his dad in style, and always made sure to keep in touch, but nothing could ever make up for lost time.

Sammy's portfolio had also managed to make him feel guilty about *her*. He'd sent her packing without a backward glance. Was he so ensconced in his ivory tower that the pleas of someone whose future he had irrevocably altered should fall on deaf ears—even when he shared a past with that person?

Of course, he wasn't going to redesign his hotel to accommodate her, which would be utter madness, but he had a couple of ideas. There was room for manoeuvre. Anybody else and he wouldn't be sitting here now, that was for sure. But memories had a funny way of finding cracks in what he'd thought was rock-solid—such as his immunity to the weakness of any emotion.

Around him, the weak winter sun was already beginning to show signs of fading away, even though it wasn't much after three in the afternoon. He half-expected no one to be in so, when he rang the bell, he was disconcerted to hear footsteps approaching. Then the door was opened just a crack, with a chain separating him from green eyes peering suspiciously at him.

'I have something you forgot.' He waved the portfolio at the four-inch crack in the door. 'Just in case you're wondering why I've shown up on your doorstep.'

'I no longer need that, so you can go away. I have nothing to say to you.'

'Look…' He raked his fingers through his hair. 'I've read your proposal—'

'And you're going to change your mind and let me buy the place so that I can open my café and develop upstairs for myself?'

'Unfortunately not.'

'Then goodbye.'

Sammy pushed the door shut and he rang the doorbell again. There was no reply. Rafael kept ringing. When she opened it yet again, he was still there, six-foot-four inches of implacable alpha male in no particular rush to leave.

She glared at him.

Rafael Moreno was the last person on the planet Sammy had expected to see standing outside her front door at three-thirty on a wintry Saturday afternoon.

She was just back from visiting her mother. She had planned to tell her everything about the hotel, and the abrupt end to all her plans for opening her patisserie, but the minute she had sat down she had looked at her mother's thin, anxious face and had immediately decided that this was a bridge she would cross at a later date.

Caroline Payne hadn't had the easiest of lives. She'd lost her husband and the father to both her children over two decades ago, and Sammy often wondered whether she had ever recovered from the loss. Seven at the time, all Sammy could remember was her mother's quiet tears as she'd gone through the motions of living, but she'd really only existed, biding her time until grief would leave her alone. Sammy and her brother had hovered like ghosts in a void. Sammy could remember a sense that she'd been waiting until things returned to normal and would be less sad and confusing.

Unfortunately, it had taken a long time for things to return to normal. Her mother had met and married someone else with undue haste, desperate to be rescued from her inability to cope. John Deeley, the manager at the factory where her mother had worked, had entered their lives with an arrogant determination to take charge. Meek and mild-mannered on the outside, he had soon proved himself to be a bully who made up for his inadequacies by throwing his weight around within the four walls of the house. Shouting and belittling her hadn't been enough to make their mother leave him; it was only when he'd raised a hand to strike Colin that she had finally snapped.

Even then, it had taken ages before he had finally disappeared from their lives and only after the police had become involved. When Sammy recalled that period in their lives, she still felt the grip of childish fear suffocate her.

Her mother had pulled herself together since those days. She'd got herself a decent job, studied in the evenings and worked her fingers to the bone to make sure she was never late with a mortgage payment. She had instilled in her only daughter the idea that men weren't the be all and end all, and that independence counted for everything.

Sammy had known as she'd matured that her mother was devoting herself to making up for those lost years when she had been wrapped up in her misery, and then later, those years when she had subjected Sammy and Colin to the horror of a stepfather like John Deeley.

Sammy had done her best to reassure her mother that time had moved on since then. It was true that Colin had gone off the rails, which her mother had taken as her fault; but he was on the straight and narrow now. Sammy repeatedly told her mother that she was happy, was fulfilled, had found her calling, but guilt and worry had taken up residence in her mother's heart and refused to budge. But, amidst all this, Caroline Payne had done her utmost financially and emotionally to support both of her children.

Working in various kitchens, training finally to branch out and do her own thing, had come at a cost to Sammy. There had been arduous hours and not much of a pay cheque. She had been grateful to her mother for the handouts she had given her over the years. She'd promised herself that she would get where she wanted to be and would repay her mum for everything she'd done for Colin and her.

So to break the news that the whole thing was off thanks to Rafael...no chance.

Which brought her right back to the man plonked outside her house, refusing to move.

'People are going to start wondering what's going on,' he had the nerve to say with a glimmer of a smile. 'If memory serves me, it's the sort of place where curtains have a habit of twitching, and the neighbours' curtains are remarkably close to yours...they've probably got their ears pressed to their front doors, even as I stand here try-ing to have a conversation.'

'I'm not interested in a conversation.'

'Let me in, Sammy. I may not have any intention of rearranging my entire project to accommodate you, but I'm willing to consider other options that could be of interest.'

'What other options?'

'Let me in and you'll find out. Slam the door and I walk away, and you won't hear from me again.'

'You can come in, Rafael, but I'm warning you that, if you don't have anything to say that I want to hear, then you won't be hanging around for longer than five seconds.'

'Consider it a deal. I've always been averse to mak-ing a nuisance of myself.' He smiled as she unhooked the chain and pulled open the front door.

That smile knocked Sammy for six. It was something that hadn't changed. It was the same smile that had had every girl in school round-eyed and mesmerised. It was a slow smile of utter self-assurance. She could see the boy he'd been very clearly.

She sighed and stood back, allowing him to sweep past her. She was only doing this because he'd held out a thread of hope when he told her that he had an idea… If not for that, naturally she would have sent him on his way, smile or no smile. She had zero interest in taking a trip down memory lane with the man.

'Do you want something to drink?'

'Graciously offered, I must say. What's on offer?'

'Tea or coffee. The coffee's instant.'

'I must say I've never had to work so hard for a drink before.'

'You can go into the sitting room—' she nodded to a door that was slightly ajar '—and I'll bring you…?'

'Tea…one sugar. That would be very nice.'

Rafael watched for a couple of seconds as she disappeared into the kitchen, kicking the door shut behind her.

Maybe she thought he might make a nuisance of himself by following her into the kitchen to talk when her mission was to get rid of him as fast as she could. No problem. As things stood, he was very happy to take his time looking round him. The unprepossessing façade outside hadn't concealed anything surprising or wonderful. The place was certainly no Tardis; it was just as small on the inside as it promised on the outside. If he stood with his arms outstretched, he would be able brush his fingers against the walls. A small staircase led upstairs. He noted the neutral paint, the faded rug on the flagstone floor and the single utilitarian light illuminating the space.

He nudged open the door to the sitting room. This was obviously where the magic happened. The bookshelves groaned under the weight of cookery books. The pictures on the walls were cute, little surrealistic depictions of food; peering closer, he could see that some were handpainted. The furniture was old but invitingly homely and the little oval table in the middle, along with a couple of other bits and pieces, was the genuine article—antique, polished so that the patina of the wood gleamed. The room was an intriguing mix of old and new.

He was studying one of the hand-painted pictures on the wall when he heard her enter the room and turned to look at her without moving.

'Yours?'

'I beg your pardon?'

'The paintings. Did you do them?'

'You should be sitting and waiting for me, not nosing around.'

'The temptation to inspect was too great. So, do you paint as well as cook?'

'When I get the time,' Sammy confirmed, nodding to a chair and pointedly placing his mug on the table next to it.

Rafael ignored her direction and took his time examining the cookery books. Some were huge; most looked very well worn.

He'd come to...what...assuage his guilt by offering her something to hang onto? Satisfy some never-before-suspected curiosity about the life he and his father had left behind all those years ago? Rafael didn't know. His entire life had been devoted to ascent. Ascent to a place where he would be untouchable. He had built a fortress around himself and that was just how he liked it. Yet here he was, with a woman who felt free to say whatever she wanted, to hell with what he thought—and, yes, he was perversely enjoying the experience. He reckoned that there was clearly more to be said for novelty than he'd ever thought possible.

'Are you going to sit or are you going to go through everything in the room with a fine-tooth comb?'

'You haven't changed. There was always a quiet determination about you, even when you were younger. Your face is the same as well. You haven't aged at all. When you left my office—or maybe it would be more accurate of me to say when you *stormed out of* my office—I began casting my mind back to those two years my father and I spent in these parts and I was surprised at what I could recall after all these years.'

'Really? How interesting…'

Her outfit the day before hadn't done her justice, he decided.

What she wore now suited her: faded skinny jeans, an old rugby shirt, likewise faded, some soft sneakers with the laces undone as though he'd caught her in the act of kicking them off. She had the smoothest skin he'd ever seen and the boyish haircut somehow managed to make her look ultra-feminine and very delicate.

'When we were at school, I remember other girls tossing their long hair over their shoulders and batting their eyelids, even though they were only about fourteen or fifteen. They were already learning the tricks of the trade.'

'The tricks of the trade?'

'How to flirt. You never did that.'

'I've never seen the point of flirting.'

'Never?'

'Can we just move things along, Rafael? Maybe get to

the point? You said that there was something you want to run past me?'

'You told me that I led your brother astray—that he was the model student before I came along and decided to show him that there was more to life than burying himself in books.'

'It was okay for you! You never had to work hard! Everything came naturally to you. You could bunk off class for days on end and then show up and know exactly what the lessons were about, exactly how to get straight As without trying.'

Sammy dropped onto the sofa facing him and looked at him with open hostility.

'I've thought about that since I saw you. I hadn't thought about it for years but it all came back to me.'

'I don't see the point of this.'

'He was very unhappy. He used to talk about it. Not a huge amount, but enough.'

'He talked to you?'

'Why is that so surprising?'

'Because…because…'

'I can be an attentive listener.'

'And you were, back then? Would that be in between taking the day off to explore the great outdoors and smoking behind the bike sheds at school?' She arched her eyebrows with incredulity and Rafael burst out laughing.

His dark eyes gleamed as he tilted his head to the side and stared at her until she blushed.

'They were tough times for you and your brother. He used to talk about a stepfather…the name escapes me.'

Sammy's mouth dropped open.

'Colin talked about Deeley...our stepfather? That all happened before you showed up!'

'I think he was still in the process of getting over it,' Rafael said quietly. 'Whatever *it* was. He was never that expansive on the subject although, in fairness, I wasn't always one hundred percent on the ball. Which brings me back to the accusation that I was a bad influence— I wasn't. I was just a catalyst for his anxieties to come out into the open. Just in case some of your annoyance that things haven't panned out the way you wanted them to might have to do with the fact that I am the Big Bad Wolf in your eyes, from a historic point of view.'

The tea had gone cold and Sammy's thoughts were all over the place.

Colin, who was three years older than her, had seemed so contained; he had seemed just to get lost in his school-work while everything had swirled chaotically around him. But was Rafael right? Had he just been there... clever, wild, non-conformist, expecting nothing...allow-ing Colin to get rid of things buried deep inside? He'd been pretty rebellious after Rafael had left, but then he'd settled down. Now that she looked back on it, something had changed—he'd mellowed.

She heard him ask very softly, into the silence, 'And what about you?'

'What about *me*?'

'It was a long time ago, but whatever disruption your stepfather caused must have affected you as well...'

And just like that Sammy was thrown back to the past—to how devastated her mother had been after Oliver Payne's death and then how hurt and disillusioned by the mess that had come of her second marriage to John Deeley.

If Rafael had developed a talent for recall, then he wasn't the only one. She could remember how she had scorned those girls who had tried so hard to get his attention and, worse, how she had hated herself for secretly being as fascinated by him as everyone else seemed to be.

He had cast a spell over them. Reluctantly, she was forced to concede that her anger at finding out who had bought the hotel and pulled the rug from under her feet was partly fuelled by him being who he was—when really he'd just been a boy who had become an incredibly successful man and now wanted to invest in a community he had once been a part of. He hadn't been personally spiteful towards *her* in buying the place she had saved up for. It had just been business for him—as he'd said.

She forced herself to meet his piercing stare with a bland expression. In the very short space of time that she had been in his company, he was already getting under her skin. She wasn't going to start spilling her heart out to him and tell him all about her miserable time when Deeley had been around. She wasn't going to revert to being the shy fourteen-year-old peering at the cute boy who could have any girl he wanted.

'We all have things in the past that have affected us one way or another,' she said politely. 'You must have stuff you'd rather not talk about, and fortunately...' she paused for dramatic effect '...I won't be asking you to tell me all about it because I'm not interested.'

'That's very, very...' Rafael's lips twitched with suppressed amusement '...reassuring.'

'So maybe we could get back to the reason you're here?'

Their eyes locked.

'What else do you do aside from baking and cooking?' he asked.

'Sorry?' Sammy was confused. Why was he avoiding getting down to the business of why he had come here in the first place?

'I read in your spiel that you trained under some big names. I take it you have experience across the board when it comes to your culinary skills? I could have looked you up online but I wanted to ask you face to face.'

'Of course. I work twice a week at a restaurant close by. It has a Michelin star and it's excellent for keeping my hand in with the basics of French and Mediterranean cooking. I also advertise my services as a personal chef, which can be extremely challenging. My heart lies in the intricacies of baking, though, which is why I've decided to start with a café that does light food and specialises in pastries. You'll appreciate that I have to make ends meet somehow. I've sacrificed quite a bit to get experience over the years. I had to work extremely long hours. Putting aside enough money for the deposit on the café has been a labour of—'

'I've got that message loud and clear. Here's the thing... I'm hosting an important series of meetings on a tiny island in the Caribbean in two weeks' time. It's a deal that involves the CEOs all coming together to dovetail the sale of several of their companies to me. But it's important that the deal is done smoothly and, most importantly, in the space of a week. I'm hosting them at one of my new hotels—it's not officially open to the public yet. There's a new restaurant in the hotel that I'm on the verge of opening. I'm willing to try you out as Head Chef while we're out there. You'll be able to show me a variety of skills.'

'Head Chef...? Small island...? Caribbean...?' She found it difficult to keep up with what Rafael was saying. The words were coming fast at her and she barely had time to pin them down. What on earth was he saying?

'Excellent weather this time of year.'

'But... I'm confused.'

'Impress me.' He leaned forward, arms resting on his thighs, giving her his undivided attention. 'And I'll hire you to steer the restaurant. You can have free rein to come up with whatever menus you like, just so long as there's an emphasis on local produce. It won't be a permanent situation—six months, the first of which will be the week of the meetings. Of course, I'll stay on after my clients have left to oversee the final touches, but I'll be out of your hair. After those six months are up, you'll be free to return here and open whatever kind of restaurant you want. You'll be paid enough so that buying a place of your own will be more than affordable. You'll also have me on your CV.'

'I'll have *you* on my CV?'

'You successfully run my restaurant in a start-up hotel, and your database of clients will be guaranteed. You just have to let it be known that you impressed me.'

They looked at one another and Sammy eventually rolled her eyes.

'You are an *extremely* arrogant human being, Rafael Moreno.'

Rafael grinned. 'I know. I'm working on it.'

'So,' she said, swiftly bringing the conversation back to logistics, because she'd been tempted to laugh. 'If the restaurant is only now in the process of…of being operational, then how is it going to be possible for me to cook anything? What's the equipment like? And how many… er…people are going to be there?'

'Twelve, including partners.'

'Okay.'

'The equipment has been ordered. You can oversee what's coming. Consider it the start of your new, exciting career.'

'And until the stuff arrives—sandwiches and barbecues on a beach?'

'That does sound reasonably relaxed,' Rafael mused. 'And relaxed is the aim of the game for the week. But, no. No sandwiches or barbecues on the beach. High-end fine dining, champagne and caviar, and interesting excursions for the other halves during the day when business is being done. I have a local guy already in place for that. You look a little bewildered.'

'Should I go along with this…? I can't just stay put over there when you and everyone else has left after the meetings are over.'

'You'll have a fortnight to return here so that you can sort out your affairs before you return. Six months isn't very long. You might think that I would want you to stay put for longer, to prove your worth before I make a decision, but…'

'But?' Sammy echoed coolly.

'But, if I'm honest, the fact that I know you in a manner of speaking changes the picture.'

'You knew me yesterday and the picture didn't seem to be changing then. If I recall, you sent me on my way because there was nothing you were willing to do for me.'

'Maybe,' Rafael admitted truthfully. 'That was an instinctive reaction. I'm not a man who is sentimental when it comes to the past, but in this instance…' He shrugged, but his eyes were serious and thoughtful. His voice became rough. 'Let's just say that I read what you'd written in your proposal and maybe I'm more sentimental than I thought. I also think you have the sort of personality to get the hotel moving in the right direction quickly.'

'And what sort of personality is that, if I could ask?'

'Argumentative and determined not to take no for an answer.'

His voice was matter of fact. There was no criticism intended, but somewhere deep inside Sammy felt a sudden stab of hurt because…were those feminine traits?

She was twenty-seven, and yes she had had boyfriends, but had any of them come to anything? No. Her last boyfriend, a guy she'd been dating for seven months, had told her, by way of an excuse for breaking up with her by text, that she was a little *difficult*.

She'd taken that to mean that her independence had ended up getting on his nerves, but what was so wrong with being independent? She had learned valuable lessons from her mother whose helplessness had been her undoing until she'd found the strength and courage to realise that going it alone was no bad thing. Worse would be to feel that she had to rely on some guy to make decisions that affected her life.

She looked at the drop-dead gorgeous man who was looking back at her with a shuttered expression and she thought of the women he was routinely pictured with. None of them looked the *difficult* type.

'I wish you'd just tell me what's missing from this picture,' Sammy said sharply, shaking her head clear of those silly, thorny thoughts. This all felt too good to be true—there had to be a catch.

'We won't be staying at the hotel,' Rafael revealed. 'It isn't due to formally open until the end of the month, which will give my managers plenty of time to ensure there are no glitches.'

'Where will we be staying? Where is this cooking going to take place?'

'At my house there. I hope you don't have a problem with that…'

CHAPTER THREE

Hope you don't have a problem with that…?

Have a problem with vanishing off to a place she'd never heard of in a part of the world she'd never visited to cook for a man she barely knew and had contrived to forget how much she didn't like? All in an attempt to prove herself worthy of being given an opportunity to find a foothold in the culinary world, because he'd thoroughly trashed her chances there when he'd gazumped her on the deal she'd made to buy the place adjoining the hotel.

Why on earth would she have a problem with that? That was what she sarcastically asked herself on a loop over the course of the following two weeks as she got herself prepared for the shake-up in her life she'd been cornered into accepting.

Bitter though she was at the olive branch that had been handed to her—because she should never have been put in the position of having to have an olive branch waved in front of her in the first place—she had to admit that he was being generous. His PA emailed her with the contract outlining what was expected of her, the duration of her employment—one week on probation followed by the six-month contract—and of course her remuneration, which was more than generous.

At the end of her stint, she would easily have sufficient capital to find herself a suitable outlet for her business and buy herself somewhere decent enough to put down roots. Those months away would be challenging, of course, because she would know no one at all and would be going it alone, in charge and without a familiar face to guide her. The fact that she could fail to make the grade after all that cast a long shadow but she had no choice to speak of and would go with the flow.

For such a hard-headed businessman, guilt certainly seemed to have sunk its teeth into Rafael; but she still couldn't manage to get herself to any place of gratitude because, generous offer or no generous offer, he was still as arrogant as he'd been as a teenager.

She was forced to confess to her mother that the deal with the hotel had fallen through and had plastered a smile on her face as she'd put as good a spin on the situation as she possibly could.

'But…you're going to…*where*—to be a personal chef because you can't get the place at Clifford's hotel? I'm just not following you. It all sounds very sketchy... I thought you *wanted* to have your own place. It's what you've spent years working towards! I just don't understand what's going on.'

Sitting across the kitchen table at her mother's house, Sammy breathed in deeply and tapped into a reservoir of phony optimism she'd never thought she possessed.

'It's a thrilling opportunity!' she trilled through gritted teeth. 'In fact, I'll bet not getting that silly place will end up being the best thing that's ever happened to me!'

'But all your plans to move upstairs so that you could own your own place as well as the bakery...'

'Oh, Mr Moreno—or *Rafael* as I call him, seeing that we know one another—will be paying me sufficiently over the six-month period at his hotel for me to have quite some choice when it comes to another venue!' She swept that observation aside, making sure not to mention the little technicality of a probationary period. Why muddy the water when her mother was actually buying into the whole change of plan?

Sammy would do anything to spare her mum needless worry and so a little finger-crossing was perfectly acceptable if it made her happy.

Oddly, having tentatively mentioned Rafael's name to find that her mother had instantly remembered who he was, the fact that *he* was the billionaire who was now giving her this so-called chance of a lifetime somehow ended up reassuring her mother that all would be okay. This, despite the fact that the odious man had been responsible for ruining her future in the first place. Sometimes Sammy just didn't understand her mother, but still, she was at least relieved that she seemed to have stopped worrying.

She got hold of as much information as she could about the Caribbean island where she might just end up spending a few months. It was small—a dot in the middle of the ocean—but with a good infrastructure and a thriving economy based on the export of sugar cane, cocoa and tourism. There were strict controls in place when it came to the number of hotels allowed, and the size of them, and there were draconian hoops to jump through for anyone not of local ancestry to get permission to own land and build on it.

Rafael's name was mentioned as being one of the lucky ones. From the write up, the journalist in question obviously loved him, and Sammy abandoned reading about all the things he had done for the islanders after the first page. He obviously had a sprawling fan club, but thankfully she had no intention ever of signing up to become a member.

She knew that he would be travelling ahead of her, which was blessed relief. But, at dawn on the day that he had arranged for the chauffeur to collect her, she was suddenly floored by an attack of nerves and almost wished that he was going to meet her at Gatwick after all.

The bravado she had nurtured over the past fortnight, when she had been busy planning what to take and preparing detailed lists of what she would need on the catering front, seemed to have deserted her. At six in the morning, with wintry dark skies outside, she scrutinised her reflection in the mirror in her bedroom and tried not to feel sick with nerves.

It was going to be hot when she got there. She would be leaving horrible weather and stepping out into hot sun—at least, according to everything she had read. When she looked at herself, what she saw was a confusing sight: light jeans and a white tee-shirt underneath a thick cardigan with a duffel coat and a woolly hat. She looked like someone who hadn't a clue where she was heading or what to expect, and so had dressed for all eventualities.

The time had come—no backing out now. Her phone buzzed: a text message from Rafael's driver, which had been the agreed communication when Rafael had arranged for her to be collected. Her lift was here. She gave one last look but, as she pulled her cases out to the front door, she wondered whether her jumbled sartorial choices reflected the jumble of emotions running through her and the confusion of not knowing what to expect when she got to the other side.

The sun had just about set as Rafael approached the airport terminal. It was easy finding a spot to park because the terminal was tiny and the car park, for reasons that escaped him, was unnecessarily large. The sky was indigo and, even though he was at an airport, he could still hear the sounds peculiar to tropical nights: the clicking of crickets blending into the background noises of frogs and toads and all the other small creatures that emerged at night.

Planes were not on a loop here. The sky was empty but, as he parked the small four-by-four, he could hear the distant roar of one swerving towards the little island, so perfectly positioned that it always escaped the annual round of hurricanes that cut a swathe through some of the other islands further north towards Puerto Rico.

He'd had minimal contact with Sammy since they'd parted company a couple of weeks ago. A contract had been emailed, conditions laid down and signatures received. He had instructed his PA to email her with some information about where she would be going, and he had personally emailed her confirming numbers and telling her that she would have to be equipped to cater for two vegetarians. In return, she had sent him a list of basics she would need including an assortment of meats, fish and prawns, which could be frozen and used as appropriate. She would get fresh stuff when she arrived. They'd been business-like communications.

He'd felt the need to put some distance between them, although he couldn't quite understand why. This was about business, and it should have been clear cut, but she'd somehow got under his skin and he hadn't been able to get her out of his head for the past couple of weeks. He'd thought of her, angrily jabbing her finger at his audacity. He'd married it to memories of her as a teenager, and had been unnerved by how much air time she'd taken in his mind.

Rafael sighed and vaulted out of the car. Perhaps he should have taken a slightly more personal approach, especially given the situation in which he had recently found himself, which had turned out to be rather delicate, to say the very least. He needed Sammy on side rather than glaring at him from under her lashes.

The airport was busy. People were coming to collect friends or relatives, others arriving to drop off. It was still very warm, even though the sun was setting, and despite a light breeze. He was half-enjoying the sing-song lilt of the voices around him as he strolled towards the pick-up point outside the little terminal. Mostly, though, he was thinking about how he was going to play this one out.

He almost missed her as she appeared through the open side of the terminal where a stream of arrivals was making its way out, pulling bags, or else with bags loaded onto trolleys being pulled by the guys who worked at the airport.

Sammy was gazing around her with a lost expression, a chunky cardigan loosely knotted around her waist, in pale-blue baggy jeans and trainers and with a couple of pull-along cases with a coat draped over the handle of one. She looked very young and very wide-eyed, the breeze riffling her short dark hair, blowing it this way and that. Their eyes met and, even in the semi-darkness, he could make out her sudden stiffening as he walked towards her.

'Sammy.'

Sammy blinked. Eight and a half hours had taken her from a cold and bleak England to…somewhere that felt like another planet. The sky was clear and the heat was seeping through her clothes, making her perspire, and the noises were ones with which she was utterly unfamiliar.

She'd been abroad, but never anywhere tropical and, the minute she'd stepped out of the plane onto the stunted ladder that led down to the tarmac, she'd been confronted with the reality of just how much was about to change for her.

Frankly, *everything*—which had fired up another flare of resentment towards Rafael, the employer she hadn't asked for and certainly didn't want. But, now that she was here and he was towering over her, he seemed like an anchor in these unfamiliar waters.

'Let me take your bags. Is this all you brought with you? Tell me how your flight was—was it okay? I find first class always makes the most of a tedious experience.'

'I didn't expect you to come and meet me.'

'That wasn't the original plan,' Rafael murmured soothingly. 'But then I thought that here you were...a stranger in a strange land and you might find it helpful to see a face you recognise.'

They were heading towards the car park. The horizon fading away into a darkening sky looked limitless...a stretch of colour uninterrupted by buildings, housing, factories or even the usual network of busy roads that led out of airport terminals.

Sammy breathed in a heady aroma of exotic trees and plants and then eyed Rafael suspiciously out of the corner of her eye.

'You're being very nice to me, Rafael.'

'I didn't realise that was a crime. Here we are. The cars here are usually driven for their usefulness, hence this four-by-four pick-up. It can tackle all manner of poor roads.'

'You mentioned that you weren't going to meet me because your contingent of guests would be at the villa. Won't they be missing you?'

'They'll all big boys and girls. They can cope for a couple of hours.'

'Is that how long it's going to take to get to your villa?' Sammy frowned and clambered into the passenger seat. 'I didn't think that the island was that big…'

'It's not. Ready?'

He swivelled so that he was facing her. Their eyes met in the darkness of the pick-up and Sammy blushed. Her comfort zone was several thousand miles and over eight hours away. She shivered, and for a few seconds her brain went completely blank because, up close and personal like this, the sheer power of his presence and the force of his incredible, suffocating masculinity hit her like a sledgehammer.

She'd spent the intervening time reminding herself that she disliked him…but now the past and the present rushed at her, giving him form and shape, and making him more than just a convenient cardboard cut-out of a bad guy.

It took her a couple of moments before her brain re-engaged and, just as he turned the engine into life and began reversing out of the space, she said, 'So why is it going to take so long?'

'Thought it might be an idea to take you somewhere… so I could brief you on what to expect.'

Sammy relaxed against the head rest and smiled.

'I think I have a pretty good idea of what to expect.'

'You do?'

'Thirteen people…'

'Fourteen, as it happens,' Rafael corrected.

'I thought you said that there were going to be six couples and a singleton.'

'My apologies. There was a last-minute addition. Clement Hewell was always scheduled to come—he's frankly the overriding lynchpin in this deal—but originally he was coming solo. As it turns out, he's accompanied by his recently acquired girlfriend, Victoria.'

'Okay. Seven couples. It shouldn't make a difference to the catering.'

'You were saying that you know what to expect. Is this on the food front or on the people front?'

'Both, as it happens,' Sammy said. She shifted so that she was leaning against the door and looking at his sharp profile. She was too tired to argue, and besides, the conversation felt soothing and non-confrontational.

She might not enjoy the reasons that had brought her here but there was something oddly invigorating about being in this man's presence. Maybe it was the challenge of proving to him how good she was at what she did—that the gauche teenager he vaguely remembered had turned out into a capable woman with a career path ahead of her. Maybe there was something gnawing away inside, something that wanted to show him that he hadn't left a bunch of country bumpkins behind in his headlong rush to become a billionaire.

The silence thickened as the pick-up gathered pace, clearing the confines of the airport and heading out into quiet, dark roads, sporadically lit and interrupted by a lazy stream of cars and vans. She realised that he was waiting for her to continue.

'On the food front, I always tend to over-cater, but

from experience when it comes to… I'm not sure how to put this…'

'Don't mind me,' Rafael murmured with amusement in his voice. 'You have to remember that I wasn't always loaded. My sensibilities are a lot less delicate than you could ever imagine.'

Sammy relaxed, something she hadn't expected to do. 'Okay. From my experience, rich people don't tend to eat a huge amount, and definitely not the wives and partners of rich men. They fiddle with their food and pick at it because they're always watching their weight.'

Rafael chuckled.

'Isn't that a generalisation?'

'Maybe,' Sammy admitted. 'But I'm just saying what I've observed over the years. So I've planned great food, keeping it nice and tasty, using local ingredients, which I've looked up, and I intend to make sure that I don't have much wastage. By the way, thanks for getting the basics in place for me. I really believe in not throwing anything out and it upsets me when I have to.'

'Very good.'

'Is that what you wanted to brief me on—picky eaters? Can I ask if everyone has arrived?'

'Two days ago.'

The darkness had gathered around them. Sammy could feel it pressing against the window of the air conditioned four-by-four. She was drawn to stare out at the passing scenery: the outcrops of houses against hills; the empty vegetable and fruit stalls by the side of the road;

the sudden bursts of lively bars and rum shops with people congregated outside, drinking and laughing.

She was also driven to look at the man behind the wheel. The longer she looked at him, the harder it was to think straight, so she dragged her eyes away and stared ahead. That was much easier.

'How's it going? Or is that none of my business?'

Rafael didn't answer.

She'd relaxed, which was good. It was difficult *not* to relax over here. There was something about the heat and the techni-colour natural beauty of the place...

Rafael made a right, heading towards the small, bustling town which struck a nice balance between being authentic and serving up some great restaurants and cafés frequented by tourists for the most part. He personally preferred the out of the way places where the locals gathered, but then he knew the place like the back of his hand, and was well known in the community.

'I know you've been up and moving for quite some time, and you're probably in need of a shower and sleep, but, like I said, er...' He fished around for the right tone of voice and the correct choice of words.

'I don't need a lesson on how to behave around your guests, Rafael. I can handle myself around people—even rich and important people, believe it or not. Experience as a personal chef is great when it comes to teaching you how to socialise, even with people you may not have much in common with and might actually dislike.'

'There's a way of doing that?' He slid dark eyes across to her.

'It involves a lot of smiling.'

'You'll have to teach me some time,' he murmured. 'I've always had a problem with that.'

'I know.' Sammy laughed. 'I remember once seeing you outside the principal's office. I have no idea what you'd done but you must have done something.'

'I was always doing *something*. Looking back, the guy had the patience of a saint...'

'Anyway, you were chewing gum and had your legs stretched out and you were playing something on your phone. You didn't look as though you were going to be smiling your way through whatever punishment was in store for you. At any rate, I'll be perfectly fine finding my feet.'

'I'm not doubting that for a second.'

'Aren't you?'

'No.' He turned to her and their eyes met briefly. 'You don't strike me as being afraid of much. You *did* show up at my office and yell at me because I'd bought the hotel from under your feet. I've probably been scarred for life.'

He grinned. 'So, no need to become defensive. I have every confidence in your culinary capabilities as well as your social *savoir faire*. I had a look at your social media profile. You've had a convincing amount of experience working in different milieu—different restaurants with different chefs, and also catering for the rich and famous. It might have been a slow climb for you but not because you haven't excelled along the way.'

'No need to over-egg the pudding,' Sammy muttered, burning with a mixture of pleasure and embarrassment.

'I'm being truthful.' The main road, such as it was, had been left behind and they were now in the capital. It was a charming mix of restaurants, bars and shops, from the sophisticated, catering for wealthy tourists, to the authentic, where the locals tended to hang out. Rafael eased the pick-up into a spare bay along a buzzing little street that was bustling with people. 'Are you always this prickly when you're paid a compliment?'

His dark eyes roved over her flushed face. 'Look,' he said softly, raking his fingers through his hair. 'What I want to talk to you about has nothing to do with…your abilities to cook or mix or anything like that. Not at all. You couldn't be further from the truth.'

'Then what?' She hesitated. 'Have you…have you decided that I won't be suitable for the…for the…?'

'Let's go inside.' He nodded to the bar directly opposite them but his eyes remained pinned to her face.

He climbed out of the pick-up, hit the passenger side before she could even open her door and rested his hand on hers to help her down because it was a crazily high vehicle.

His fingers were cool against hers and sent a tingle through her as he touched her. *What was going on…?*

Sammy had expected a number of things, starting with sickening nerves, disorientation and borderline panic, all mingled with a healthy dose of sourness and resentment. She hadn't expected to feel at all relaxed, not at any point; nor had she expected to see any funny side to Rafael and she certainly hadn't expected him to be... *hesitant* with her about anything.

And yet, she had *sensed* his hesitancy when he had brought her here and suddenly she realised that she wanted this job a lot more than she had told herself. She'd worked and worked and worked to get this far and she couldn't face any more setbacks in her quest to forge her own path. She didn't *want* to have to start thinking about putting aside more money so that she could find somewhere else, somewhere that wouldn't be half as suitable as the hotel, which was no longer even a possibility.

She'd subconsciously started making plans with the money he had dangled in front of her, even though she had fought against the temptation; she had hung onto the reality that there would still be a probationary period to climb over, not to mention the sickening prospect of being on this island on her own, making decisions that would affect her future. Bracing lectures to herself could only go so far.

She nervously detached from him as soon as her feet hit the ground. 'So, want to tell me what's going on?' she asked.

Silhouettes of palm trees swayed all around them, a thick, dense forest leading to the sea; it wasn't visible yet, but she could tell it was there from the salty aroma in the air. The stars were tiny, glittering diamonds in a velvety black sky and the warmth penetrated even her thin tee-shirt and the loose jeans. Even the fact that they were in a bar couldn't detract from the dramatic splendour of their surroundings. In the darkness, all she could make out was Rafael's powerful build and his chiselled facial features.

'What's going on is that there's a slight spanner in the works.' Rafael cleared his throat.

'Meaning? Look, if you're having second thoughts about taking me on after this stint, then that's fine. There's no need to think that I'm going to take you to court because of a stupid contract.'

'Point of order—you couldn't. The contract stipulates complete freedom for me to release you without obligation should I no longer think that you can handle the six-month part of the job at my hotel. Didn't you read the fine print, Sammy?' He shook his head. 'Anyway. This isn't to do with that. It's to do with…how can I put this?…a certain delicate situation that's, er, arisen concerning one of the guests at my villa…'

'I beg your pardon?'

'Let me get you something to drink. They do an excellent rum punch here.'

He ordered drinks and nibbles while Sammy looked at him in utter bewilderment. She was barely aware of a cocktail being put in front of her or of the plate of nibbles. He'd told her that whatever he had to say had nothing to do with her contract but, in that case, for the life of her she couldn't work out where this was going.

'The couple I mentioned… Clement Hewell and the woman he's brought with him…'

'Yes…?'

'He's an important player in this particular game. He

needs to be persuaded into parting with the company because, without him, the various other IT and software companies would find it hard to amalgamate. His company has certain software programmes that are vital for the whole tie-up to be possible, and that means a lot, because a lot of jobs depend on this deal. Without his contribution, the deal falls apart, and with it two of the companies, which will splinter, and that will affect a lot of people's livelihoods. The climate's not great for job hunting, and I personally know of the dozens that will be let go if this doesn't go through; most are nearing retirement age and would struggle to find anything else.'

'That's just awful, Rafael, but I honestly don't know where you're going with this.'

'The woman hanging on Clement's arm? As luck would have it, I actually know her.'

'Which is a good thing?'

'Which is very much *not* a good thing.'

'But surely catching up…?'

'Clement is a decent, honourable guy in his seventies. I've met him over the years at social events. He's well known in financial circles as a mover and shaker, who's also honest, fair and extremely generous when it comes to giving to charity.'

'That's really good to hear…but I'm really not sure where you're going with this.'

'Victoria,' Rafael expanded, 'is a twenty-nine-year-old ex-catwalk model.'

There was a moment of puzzlement, then Sammy

relaxed and grinned. Then she burst out laughing, her green eyes lighting up with genuine mirth.

'I get it.'

'Tell me.'

'She's an ex-girlfriend of yours.'

'From four years ago.' Rafael shifted uncomfortably. 'A brief liaison.'

'No need for details.' She was still grinning. 'That's not the end of the world, though, is it? Haven't you been out with lots of catwalk models in the past?'

'What makes you say that?'

'I've caught the occasional article.'

'You mean you've been stalking me?'

'Don't flatter yourself,' she said drily. 'I read the occasional tabloid and I've seen the occasional picture. Not my fault there are reporters around who can't think of anything better to do with their time than take photos of you and whatever woman you happen to be going out with.'

'Ouch.'

'What I'm saying is,' she said loftily, 'is it's hardly a crime for an ex to go out with someone else and for you to bump into them later on as a couple—although the age difference *is* a little concerning.'

'If only it was that easy,' Rafael said, the grin fading, his voice quiet and deadly serious. 'The first day was okay, but last night there was a knock on my door. I opened it to find her standing outside in a bathrobe with nothing on underneath. I managed to get rid of her, but this could prove to be a very worrying situation. It's not just the nightmare of having to be on the alert twenty-four-seven, and it's not even the inconvenience of a situation arising that might be seen as compromising through no fault of my own...'

'Meaning?'

'Meaning,' Rafael said wryly, 'she's caught flinging herself at me and whoever happens to be around leaps to an incorrect conclusion. I can't say I care what people think of me but, like I said, this is a very big deal and a lot is riding on it. I'd rather not risk Victoria getting it into her head to scupper it if she can through sheer malice. Clement is in a fragile place at the moment, recovering from the death of his wife a year ago, and old men in fragile places can sometimes be foolish. From the looks of it, he's in the foolish phase, besotted with the damn woman. He'll come to his senses, but this couldn't be a worse time for this to be happening. What I'm saying is, if Victoria gets it into her head to use her influence to spite me because I've rejected her, well, let's just say there will be some very desperate casualties looking for jobs they probably won't easily find.'

'Why don't you just tell her that you're not interested? Why would she be spiteful? Surely if you explain...?'

'It was something of a messy break up.'

'Are you saying that she wanted to hang on in there after you'd given her her marching orders?'

'That's quite a colourful way of putting it, but essentially, yes.'

'So she's still got feelings for you.'

'So it would appear.'

'I get your point. People do crazy things when they're vulnerable and your friend...well, you say he's vulnerable, but still, I'm not sure why you're telling me this when it doesn't involve me. Unless you want me to take her under my wing in the kitchen and teach her how to make puff pastry to take her mind off vengeful thoughts? Puff pastry will do that to a person.'

The joke fell flat.

'Actually.' Rafael suddenly looked uncomfortable, uncomfortable enough for Sammy to feel a shiver of apprehension thread through her. 'This concerns you a little more than you might expect.'

'How so?'

'Because you and I are an item...'

'I beg your pardon?'

'Practically engaged, as it happens. Just for the week, you and I are very much in love. It was the only way I could get her off my back...'

CHAPTER FOUR

FOR A FEW seconds Sammy thought she must have missed a crucial link somewhere. How had Rafael's dilemma suddenly become *her* problem? Her mouth dropped open and she stared at him, oblivious to a smiling waiter with a jug of punch topping up their glasses.

'Hence my reason for waylaying you,' Rafael volunteered into the yawning silence.

'Rafael,' Sammy was constrained to enquire, 'How has *your* problem become *my* problem?'

'I'm not proud that I've dragged you into this but on the spur of the moment, and with that woman standing in front of me at two in the morning, my options seemed limited. I told her to get lost or I'd see what Clement makes of her after-hours escapades and she immediately warned me not to try reporting back—said all she was looking for was a bit of closure for herself. Like I said, Sammy, Victoria has a vindictive streak and if she wants to cause chaos she'll make sure to do so—she would try and spin some fairy story to Clement and, trust me, the story would not be in my favour. But if I have a serious girlfriend in tow? She wouldn't dare try and there would be no risk to the deal being done.'

'But…'

'Hear me out.' He pushed the half-empty plate of nibbles to one side and leaned towards her, his fingers linked on the table, his whole presence swamping her.

'Do I have a choice?'

'I realise that this was possibly not what you were expecting…'

'*Possibly not what I was expecting?* Rafael, that's the understatement of the decade! I was expecting an oven, a hob and a non-stop round of food preparation!'

'So, it might be a brief with a slight difference, but I'll make it more than worth your while.'

'Really. And how exactly are you going to achieve that?'

'I'm prepared to…er…alter the terms and conditions of the agreement we had in place.'

'You're losing me.'

'No working here for six months, no probationary period. I know you were probably a little apprehensive about having to prove yourself in unfamiliar surroundings…were you? Maybe you were excited at the opportunity…'

'No probationary period? What does that mean? No working here for six months? And, just for the record, more apprehensive than excited, as it happens. Six months on an island where I don't know anyone…'

'Naturally, you would have been introduced to the various people at the hotel.'

'Like I was saying…where I don't know anyone, at

the end of which I could have been found wanting, didn't exactly make for a relaxing prospect.'

'Look, it's a big ask. I know that. Work with me here and I'm prepared to release you from any commitment to prove your worth to me. When this stint is over, you leave here with a cheque in your hand and the where-withal to advance your career however you want to.' He reached for his mobile, typed something in and pushed the phone towards her.

Sammy's mouth, already open, opened a lot wider. In fact, her jaw hit the ground. The figure he had typed in was eye-watering and she wondered whether he had accidentally hit too many noughts by mistake.

'You're buying me.'

'In a manner of speaking. But look at it this way: what I'm buying is just a week of make-believe from you. You're my personal chef, an old friend who's now my lover… You'll still do the catering, and you can mingle on the side-lines as befits the working woman that you are. We really won't be spending much time in one an-other's company. You'll be preparing food and I'll be working to get this deal done before it can be scuppered. I refuse to let malice destroy the lives of innocent people who are depending on this.'

Sammy's brain had got stuck on the word 'lover' and she felt slow heat crawl into her cheeks. She tried to think of herself in that role; her mouth went dry and her thoughts became a big, scrambled mess.

'I get it that you're horrified.'

'This is not what I was expecting. Like I said…'

'In the big scheme of things, a week is neither here nor there. I won't expect anything from you but a bit of acting and, like I just said, you'll probably be busy preparing food so the acting will be limited—a smile here, a fond glance there. I'm not a touchy-feely person at the best of times.'

'And your important business colleagues are going to buy into you falling madly in love with an impoverished chef you happened to know when you were a kid?' She shot him a look of blazing disbelief. 'They surely must know that you date models and...gorgeous blonde women with big hair and long legs?'

'Well if *they* don't, then you certainly seem to.'

'No one will believe you for a second, Rafael.'

'I'll say straight away that Victoria did.'

'Well...'

'In a lot of ways, it's far more convincing that, after a string of unsuitable beauties, I've lost my heart to...'

'The girl next door? Or should I say *the girl who used to be next door*? Thanks for the compliment.'

'To a girl who's the complete opposite of what I've always gone for—to a proud and ambitious working woman who isn't interested in living a life of leisure, whiling away her time doing her nails and shopping for designer clothes.'

'Which is what the women you date enjoy doing?'

'I've never had a problem with that. At any rate, being a full-time model involves more than nail-doing and designer-clothes shopping.'

'Of course,' Sammy agreed dutifully. 'Who could disagree with that?' She was half-thinking about the temptation of taking him up on an offer that could open a million doors for her and would certainly solve all her financial problems for the foreseeable future, if not for ever. If she *did* agree to his crazy scheme, would that make her easily bought or incredibly canny?

'It's an impossibly tall story to pull off, Rafael. What does this ex of yours look like?'

'Six foot one, blonde hair, long legs.'

'Exactly! Now look at *me*.'

'I'm looking.' He paused just long enough for her to blush. 'Why are you so touchy?'

'I'm not touchy! I'm being realistic.'

'Look,' Rafael said gravely. 'For the reasons I've outlined to you, I really would like you to play along with me for the next few days. Like I said, once it's under our belt, you will walk away a wealthy woman with the career opportunities you dreamed of within your reach *immediately*—no need to spend six months on an unfamiliar island.'

The carrot dangled tantalisingly. It was a truly astronomical amount of money on offer. Maybe to him it was less than a drop in the ocean, but to her? Yes, all those career opportunities would be firmly within her reach, and more besides. She would be able to treat her mother to all the things she deserved after a lifetime of scrimping and saving for her kids.

Rafael was right. What were a few days in the grand scheme of things? It would all be just a game, and one rooted in good intentions at that. Rafael would be spared the inconvenience of an ex-lover making a play at him behind her husband's back, and Sammy would get to skip the six-month stay and head straight home to Yorkshire to achieve her dream of starting her own restaurant.

'I'm tired,' she said truthfully. 'It's been a long day.'

'Let's go.' He stood up immediately and she followed suit.

The utter madness of this man being her lover flashed through her head. But then, her mind veered off on a tangent and began playing with all sorts of inappropriate images that made her burn up inside. Images of him touching her…looking at her with those clever, dark eyes…seeing more than just a nuisance who had shown up at his office clutching her portfolio and calling his conscience into question.

It was madness, of course. Rafael Moreno would never see her in that light. Men tended to go for women who were clones of one another. He went for catwalk models, or at least women who *could be* catwalk models. He was the guy who could have anyone.

'How long do I have to think about this?'

'The duration of the car ride back to my villa.'

'And if I say no?'

'Then you say no.'

'What would you tell your ex, after you've said that we're an item?'

They were walking towards his car, a warm breeze rustling her hair. She's spent hours travelling and yet she couldn't have felt more alert.

Alongside her, Rafael's towering presence made her

shiver. She threw a sideways glance at him and all she could take in was formidable, sexy masculinity which made her think back to the fascination that had held her in its grip all those years ago. Thank God times had changed and she had grown up.

He helped her into the pick-up, swerved round to the driver's side and, as soon as he was next to her, she repeated her question, curious to hear his answer.

Rafael murmured with a shrug, 'I'd tell her that we had an argument and were no longer an item. Then I'd just have to take my chances and work things out another way, if such a way exists. And, if old guys get laid off in the process, that would be something my conscience would have to come to terms with.'

He angled his body back against the door, one arm resting lightly on the steering wheel, so that he could look at her.

'Wow,' Sammy said. 'That would be a speedy break-up. One minute you've told her that we're all loved up, and the next minute, it's all over?'

'Not that unusual.'

'I always thought that things just drifted along until one day it all fizzled out...'

'Maybe for you. Is that how it's worked for you, Sammy? On the relationship front?'

'I didn't think we were talking about me.'

It suddenly felt hot and stifling in the car. Her heart picked up pace as their eyes remained locked. He'd started the engine but rolled the windows down so that fresh air blew through but, even so, she could feel her clothes tight and prickly against her skin.

'For me,' Rafael drawled, 'break-ups tend to be a little more abrupt. I'm not a great believer in the gradual fizzling out of a situation. I'm inclined to restlessness before the boredom sets in.' He waited a few seconds and then said matter-of-factly, 'Victoria would have no trouble believing that what was working one minute suddenly failed to work the next.'

He began reversing out of the space. Outside, people were coming and going, walking slowly, laughing loudly and having fun.

'And the reason for that speed-of-light change of direction?'

'You suddenly started trying to pin me down,' Rafael said without batting an eye.

'Wait. Me—try to pin *you* down? Just for the record, that may pass muster with your ex as a reason for a swift break-up, but I can't think of a single one of my friends who would ever fall for that as an excuse for this unlikely relationship coming to an end!'

'So isn't it a good thing that we don't have to convince your friends?'

'I mean,' she continued, 'does that happen often with you, Rafael? Women trying to *pin you down*?'

'It's been known to happen.' Rafael looked at her, head tilted to one side. 'Women not understanding that I'm a free agent, utterly uninterested in settling down, even though that's something I always make clear at the start of any relationship. I don't do commitment. So, trying to pin me down? Always a reason for me to walk away. Never tried to pin a guy down, Sammy?'

'No,' she scoffed.

'Then what a good match we are.'

'You say you don't *do* commitment. Don't you believe in love?'

'I don't believe that this conversation is going anywhere. Have you decided?'

Sammy blinked and grounded herself back in the here and now.

'What if something goes wrong with this so-called failsafe plan?'

'Nothing will go wrong. You and I are going out and it's the only way she'll get the message that she needs to keep out of my way.' His voice became husky, the only real indication that the favour he was asking meant more to him than he had volunteered. 'A handful of days, Sammy, and then your life changes for ever...'

'Okay.' She breathed in deeply. 'I'll do it.'

Rafael hadn't been lying when he'd told Sammy that he'd suddenly found himself in a place from where, faced with an ex naked under a bathrobe with a crazy desire for *closure* via a bit of sex behind her husband's back, the only exit strategy he could think of was to involve her.

The arrival of Victoria, latched onto her much shorter and much, much older new love interest, had sent a shiver of apprehension through him. Even so, he'd greeted them both warmly and ushered them into his villa to meet the other assembled guests without a flicker of concern on his face. At his most optimistic, he'd hoped that she wouldn't be a nuisance. At his least, he'd wondered just how destructive she might turn out to be.

Truth was, theirs had been a messy break-up. Very quickly into their relationship he had discovered that she was a fragile and vulnerable woman who needed therapy a lot more than she needed him. He had done his best to encourage her into getting help but, the harder he'd tried, the more clingy she'd become and in the end, when her calls had come in every five minutes, he'd had no choice but to begin the process of detangling himself from her.

She hadn't forgiven him but she *had* eventually disappeared from his life and he had breathed a sigh of relief. To be confronted with her now was a nightmare.

He glanced sideways at Sammy who was beginning to nod off against the door. If he could have waited until she was rested in the morning to have the conversation, he would have.

As things stood… Yes, in a sense he'd bought her, as she'd said, but not just because of the reasons he'd given her, although those were all valid. He'd offered her everything he knew she wouldn't be able to resist because, after all, he was the root cause of all her problems. It seemed that, when it came to guilty consciences, she was very good at making him rediscover the one he'd assumed he'd buried. Something about her reminded him of a time when he hadn't yet become the hard, invincible guy he was now. She was a memory of days spent raging against the world whereas now, as an adult, he no longer raged against what he had learned to control.

He half-smiled as he heard the soft sound of her breathing and, when he looked at her, it was to see that she was fast asleep.

Sammy surfaced as the pick-up slowed and then stopped. For a few seconds she was disoriented, without a clue where she was, but she remembered fast enough as she straightened and glanced sideways at Rafael's profile.

A trip that hadn't been straightforward to start with had morphed into something she couldn't have anticipated in a million years.

He killed the engine and turned to her.

'We're here, Sleeping Beauty.'

'I didn't intend to fall asleep.'

'Travel has a way of catching up with a person. Still on board for…?'

'For pretending to be the couple we aren't? I suppose so.' She heaved a heartfelt sigh. 'It would be great to leave here with a plan going forward. Is there…anything I should know before we begin this charade, aside from the fact that your ex has suddenly appeared on the scene? Should we agree on where we met? How we've ended up here in this unlikely position?'

'That's the beauty of this plan,' Rafael assured her. 'We have history. There's no need to make anything up. We met accidentally after years apart, discovered a connection as we travelled down memory lane and, hey presto.'

'It all sounds so easy if you ignore the glaring holes in the story.'

'Let's not focus on the glaring holes. I find it pays to think positive.'

'So we meet, chat about old times and suddenly it's love at first sight and marriage on the cards?'

'Crazy love. Isn't it what the world wants to believe?'

'I'm thinking only an idiot would believe that a guy like you would be a victim of *crazy love.*'

'That's because you probably know me better than anyone who's here. After all, we *do* go back a way, and you *do* have fond memories of me as a teenager to fall back on. Crazy love was definitely not my motto for the day.'

'Yes, but…'

'Don't dwell on the details. Leave it to me to do the convincing.'

Sammy couldn't tear her eyes away from his darkly handsome face. She vaguely thought that stuff that seemed too easy to be true always turned out a mess, but that thought didn't have time to grow legs before he broke eye contact and pushed open his door.

Sammy blinked and actually began to pay attention to her surroundings. She'd slept her way through a drive up a hill and emerged from sleep to an avenue of coconut trees behind her and a courtyard fringed with trees and bushes ahead. Everything was lit with the same beautiful fairy lights that had lit up the terrace where they had earlier sat with their rum punches.

His villa sat squarely off the courtyard. She had envisaged something with a sprawling wooden veranda and a hammock or two, but she couldn't have been more wrong. Instead, it was a solid white house, very, very large, set on two floors, the entrance guarded by two columns that spiralled up both floors to the terracotta roof. It nestled amidst the trees and was uber-modern in its sharp angles and uncompromising lack of frilliness. This was the villa of a guy who didn't have a romantic bone in his body.

Nerves kicked in fast and she was almost glad of the steadying hand that reached to usher her out of the pick-up, then stayed on her arm as they made their way to the front door.

'Don't stress,' Rafael murmured, flipping a key from his pocket and sliding it into the door. 'It's going to be just fine, trust me. The partners will be out during the day doing things on the island; I got my PA to arrange a series of activities to keep them busy. The business associates will be locked away discussing all the complexities of the deal I'm trying to navigate. Dovetailing several companies so that they become one takes a lot of time and patience, hence the fact that we're all here instead of in a hotel somewhere. We need to focus and relax at the same time. You'll be in a pretty amazing kitchen, working some magic with food while everyone else is busy elsewhere. Couldn't be an easier scenario.'

'Let's agree to disagree on that.'

Before she could continue, he'd pushed open the door and, on cue, someone appeared to fetch her bags from the pick-up and bring them through.

It was after eight in the evening and she could hear the rumble of noise coming from somewhere towards the back of the villa beyond the hall in which they were now standing.

He'd released her but now it was her turn to grip his arm. She was aware of magnificent furnishings as they made their way through the villa, all white. It should have looked sterile but the white was interrupted by flamboyant tropical paintings on the walls and the rich lustre of expensive rugs on the marble floor. It seemed to go on for ever as they passed various rooms, again all white, all housing local paintings and sculptures. There were various rooms for various purposes. She felt she'd stepped between the covers of a very high-end interior design magazine.

'Where's everyone?'

'Outside—dinner is served poolside. The plan is for you to briefly meet everyone and then retire: jet lag, et cetera et cetera. I expect after the day you've had you won't be arguing with that.'

'After the past few weeks I've had,' Sammy said, 'I could sleep for the next hundred years.'

'Sammy.' Rafael stopped dead in his tracks and turned, stilling her with his hand on her arm. 'The Yorkshire hotel…that was business.'

'I get that, but you must have known that I had made an offer on the side building?'

'I knew, but it wasn't a consideration when I decided to outbid you. Business is business, after all. Besides, I had no idea who had offered on the outbuilding. It wasn't my concern.'

'Would it have made you stop and think if you'd known that it was me?'

'No.'

'When did you get so hard, Rafael?'

'That's a big question for eight-thirty on a Thursday evening.'

'Does that mean that you don't want to answer?'

'It means that, whatever our game entails, questions about my personal life are off-limits.'

Sammy shrugged, but her green eyes were still curious and steady as they collided with his.

'Okay. And, just for the record, questions about mine are off-limits as well.'

'Good. Glad that's settled. Great match, like I've said. Is it any wonder we're rushing recklessly into marriage when we get one another so well? Now, shall we meet the assembled party?'

But, as they strolled through the villa, heading out towards the massive infinity pool that was perched on manicured grounds leading down to a private cove, Rafael could feel his curiosity about her pique. He'd warned her off thinking that, because they were in this unusual situation, she was somehow owed access to his private thoughts or to the things that had made him the man he was: the hurt, anger and disillusionment that had struck during his formative years, emotions never to be forgotten. No one would ever have access to that part of him.

It was fair enough that she had laid down the same ground rules for him as he'd laid down for her, and really, since when had he ever been curious about any woman's back story? So he was surprised to find himself wondering about the woman by his side with her chin held high and grim determination plastered on her face.

The sound of laughter was getting louder the nearer they got to the sprawling French doors that led out to the terrace and pool area at the back of the villa. The nights drew in early here but it remained warm enough for people to swim at night if they cared to. He never did.

He could feel her stiffen next to him. Good Lord, could she look more as though she were being dragged to face a hangman's noose?

Some nerves were understandable. He'd understand a shy smile, perhaps, as he introduced her to people she didn't know…and maybe, just maybe, an adoring look up at him… Was that asking too much?

When he glanced down, it was to see the last thing she seemed likely to give would either be adoration or a shy smile. Her mouth was pursed, her eyes were narrowed and her posture was rigid. This wasn't a woman in love with him. This was a woman who wanted to hit him over the head with a rolling pin.

He sighed to himself. There was only one thing for it. He turned to her and called her name in a low whisper. As she looked up at him, he cupped the nape of her neck with his hand, tangled his fingers into her short, dark hair and kissed her.

That kiss…

It was the last thing Sammy had been expecting. The mouth that covered hers was cool, the tongue that probed was moist and the reaction she had was devastatingly powerful. She was so surprised that she didn't pull back; so stunned that she lost herself in it and yielded to a drowning sensation quite unlike anything she had ever felt before in her life.

She tiptoed to return the kiss and her hand crept along his neck and curved the shape of his jaw just as he pulled away and murmured with husky amusement, 'Thank you.'

In a heartbeat, she realised what had just happened. About to introduce the love of his life, and fearing that *love* was probably the last thing on her face, he had pulled her to him and kissed her…kissed her until she'd been soft, compliant and rosy-cheeked…*kissed her senseless*…until she'd displayed all the classic signs of a woman in love: pink cheeks, parted lips and dazed eyes.

Blinking like an owl, she turned to a collection of very appreciative faces. Some people were standing, some were lounging on recliners and a couple was actually in the pool. The backdrop of a starry night, the dark shadows of swaying coconut trees and in the distance the even darker strip of ocean made the scene look almost staged—especially as everyone seemed to have stopped whatever they'd been doing.

'Let me introduce you to Sammy.'

Rafael's voice snapped her out of her stupor and she duly plastered a smile on her face. Her eyes were adjusting to the darkness, the lights mounted on the wall behind them picking out over-sized planters with bamboo bursting up, several sun loungers with canopies that were the size of single beds and a shaded area, beneath which was a long table and chairs and a bar area. The pool itself was absolutely enormous, flat, shiny and still.

It could only have been a matter of seconds, but it felt as though it took for ever before the silence was broken by a woman slow-clapping and stepping out of the pool.

'I never thought I'd see the day when the inveterate bachelor decided to join the ranks of us in love...' came a low, amused, husky female drawl with just the tiniest thread of bitter rage detectable, Sammy was sure, only to Rafael and her. Because of course the woman in question emerging out of the water could only be his ex.

She was an Amazonian beauty with long, long blonde hair piled on her head in an artfully tousled bun and with a figure made for wearing very, very little. That was precisely what she happened to have on: a tiny bikini that left precious little to the imagination.

She took her time wading up the shallow steps and moved to stand behind a plump, elderly man sitting at a table with a couple of other, slightly younger, guys.

'Happens to all of us in the end,' Rafael said politely.

Sammy felt the weight of his arm slung over her shoulders and, because she'd taken an instant dislike to the woman, she linked her fingers through Rafael's and smiled, her smile as polite as Rafael's response had been.

He raised her hand to his mouth and grazed her knuckles with his lips. Sammy thought that it was a tremendous performance for the guy who didn't do touchy-feely. Her brain said that. Her body, however, blazed in instant response and she knew that colour was again crawling into her cheeks.

On wicked impulse, she slid her hand along his back and then dipped her finger beneath the waistband of his jeans and got a kick when she felt his body stiffen. She smiled and wriggled her wandering finger under the shirt to feel hard, muscled skin before slowly removing her hand.

Then she was being introduced to everyone.

'I told her that there was no need for her to sweat over a stove, cooking for us all when she got here,' he crooned, arm still firmly in place, this time with his hand just below the small swell of her breast. 'But...' He turned to her and kissed the tip of her nose. 'You insisted, didn't you, my darling?'

'I did, indeed... I plan on setting up my own restaurant, and practice is always going to make perfect. Practising on a captive audience for a few days couldn't suit me better!'

For fifteen minutes, doing the rounds, she was able to make some judgements on the group of people she would be deceiving for the next few days. There were seven men, aged between about forty to the oldest, Clement, who was in his seventies. The seven women were mostly in their forties and fifties, with the exception of Victoria, who was a mere year or two older than her.

Rafael still had his arm slung over her shoulders. He was still fully playing to the audience, and it was wreaking havoc with her composure.

She yawned and edged away just a little. There was

only so much her blood pressure could take with this game of make-believe.

'Come along, darling, time for bed,' Rafael crooned and Sammy looked up at him with a suitably adoring expression. She batted her lashes; he grinned and in return dipped his head to kiss her again. This time his tongue flicked between her parted lips and her breathing hitched. He pulled back with a convincing sigh of regret.

Just as soon as they hit the stairs, she pulled away from him and glared, because he was grinning.

'Convincing acting,' he murmured, leading the way.

'I thought you weren't the touchy-feely sort. What choice did I have but to respond in kind?'

'Very true.'

'It's why you're paying me so much money, isn't it?'

'I don't like it when you put it like that.' Rafael frowned.

'Too bad. It's all just an act and I'm fine playing make-believe when we have to.' Her body was trying hard to agree with that infuriated statement but, when their eyes met, hers were cool and composed.

He nudged open one of the doors at the very end of the landing, outside which was a seating area complete with plants and a window overlooking the back.

Sammy stopped dead in her tracks. In the middle of the room were soft chairs and a sofa interrupted by a low, square coffee table in the middle. There was a sideboard, a bar and a business-like desk that drew the eye to French doors opening out to a warmly lit veranda. Through another door to the side, she could glimpse the bedroom.

'We're sharing a bedroom,' she said flatly, folding her arms and gazing at her luggage waiting for her just outside the bedroom door. The door was ajar, and she couldn't see the bed through it, but she was guessing that there weren't conveniently going to be two singles.

'It's a thing in this day and age when two people are going out and in love.'

'We're neither.'

'Sammy, perhaps I should have warned you, but I thought you'd probably work that one out without any help from me.' He turned round, shoved his hands in his pockets and looked at her. Just those dark eyes resting on her reminded her of the kiss that had shaken her to the core and then, hard on the heels of *that* memory, *why* he had kissed her in the first place.

'Don't worry,' he said wryly. 'You can have the bed. I'm happy to take the sofa out here. As you can see, it's plenty big enough for me, even though I'm not small.'

'You could have said that from the start.'

'I know, but it's fun watching you blush.'

'This isn't about *fun*.'

'I know.' He raised his eyebrows and stared at her with his head tilted to one side, still half-smiling. 'On a practical note, I think we managed to pull off the business of you working your fingers to the bone while you're here instead of relaxing and enjoying time out with the others…or with me…even though we're crazy about one another and can't bear to be apart.'

'Being a personal chef doesn't allow for much free time.'

'So you made clear to everyone there. Who'd have

thought that making puff pastry could consume half a day? Well played, though, I must admit. No one will question you, although you might find that you have visitors popping in now and again. Perhaps you shouldn't have made it sound quite so interesting.'

'As long as Victoria isn't one of the visitors, then that's fine.'

'Who knows? You might find that I make an appearance just to catch up on how a roux gets made...'

'Ha ha.'

'Seriously, though, Sammy—thank you for this evening. Only a few more days left and life can get back to normal.'

She heaved a heartfelt sigh. 'I can't wait.'

CHAPTER FIVE

THE SUITE TURNED out fine. Sammy stepped into a bedroom the size of a football field with an adjoining bathroom. True to his word, Rafael decamped outside, taking whatever clothes he wanted with him and telling her that there was another bathroom off the sitting area which he would be more than happy to use.

'Where would I have stayed if this situation hadn't arisen?' Sammy had asked with genuine curiosity.

'The place has six bedroom suites, and four more in an annex beyond the pool, which is actually where Clement and Victoria are staying, as well as two other couples. You would have stayed in one of the suites in the main house here, simply because access to the kitchen would have been more convenient.

'Don't feel you have to rush to prepare anything for breakfast, by the way. I think that would be beyond the call of duty, considering you're supposed to actually want to lie in with me every morning rather than hurtling out of bed at six to bake bread. Might raise a few eyebrows if you really *are* buried in the kitchen twenty-four-seven when we should, theoretically, be enjoying some down time together—lazy mornings before the day has had time to kick off. Not my thing, but expectations might be high from our assembled guests, especially after last night's performance.'

'Shame. Early starts baking would have worked. My bread skills are second to none.'

'I'm sure I'll get to sample some of your creations at some point. Right now, though…no need to rush downstairs. I'll stay in the suite as well, although I'll be up and working by seven.'

Rafael lowered his eyes but he was alert to her graceful movements as she strolled towards one of the two cases she had brought, flipping it open and rifling through the contents before stepping back, folding her arms and looking at him pointedly.

'Don't worry, I'm on my way out.' He yanked back from the brink his thoughts of those casual touches earlier on. 'I think it might be a good idea if you join me for breakfast tomorrow.'

'Why?'

'Because for starters I'll have to make sure evidence of my overnight stay on the sofa is well and truly out of sight. Housekeepers can sometimes have loose tongues, and there are currently four of them doing the rounds. Might be a headache if it gets out that the lovebirds aren't sharing the bedroom. Besides, I'll drive you into town. You'll need to pick up provisions, and there's an excellent food market in the centre of the capital. I made sure the basics are all in place but you might want to see what fresh produce is out there. You'll find it all quite different from what you're used to, I'm guessing.'

'I'm excited to see what's available,' Sammy admitted. 'I spent some time looking up what I might expect and I've got a couple of ideas up my sleeve.'

'Nothing too elaborate, I hope.'

'Why?'

'I wouldn't want to have to hunt you down behind a pile of recipe books...'

'You could always avoid that by joining me behind them,' Sammy said sweetly, but then reddened when his eyebrows shot up at the unintended innuendo behind her perfectly innocent, perfectly sarcastic remark. 'What I *meant* was, I expect there's no chance of that when you've probably never cooked a home-made meal in your life.'

'Tut-tut. That's what I'd call a sweeping generalisation.' He grinned. 'You'd be surprised how many I've cooked, actually, but that's a conversation for another day. For the moment, time for us both to retire to our respective sleeping quarters. And Sammy?'

'Yes?'

'I just want to make sure that you're entirely comfortable with what we're doing.'

'In what way?'

'A fake relationship. It comes with certain strings...'

'Strings?'

'Being touched...it's expected. Were you uncomfortable with that earlier?'

His voice swirled round her like honey and she felt herself begin to burn from the inside out. When she thought of the heavy warmth of his arm draped over her...and, worse, the feel of his cool lips on hers...her pulse went into overdrive and she wanted to pass out. She didn't have his level of experience, which was something she hadn't taken into account.

Mouth dry, she managed to croak, 'No. Why should I?'

'Good. Just wanted to ask, but actually, I didn't think you were.'

'How so?'

'If you were, let's just say you wouldn't have got into the rhythm so effortlessly.'

'Yes…yes, I did do that. Get into the rhythm…effortlessly.'

'You certainly did.' His voice was approving. 'No one could have doubted our relationship when you slipped two of your fingers under the waistband of my trousers.' He grinned. 'Even *I* was a little shocked at just how much we were in love at that point.'

'Like I said, all part of the deal we made. You can rest assured that I'm fine with what has to be done. It's for an audience and, like you say, that audience isn't going to be watching twenty-four-seven.'

'Ample time to recharge your batteries in between sets,' he murmured with amusement.

He was so cool about it, so matter of fact. He'd touched her and she'd gone up in flames. She'd touched him and he'd been startled at her audacity. She wondered whether he thought that, in the back of beyond, all she got up to were barn dances, holding hands, and kissing under the mistletoe at Christmas.

'Ample time,' she agreed crisply. 'And now, if you don't mind…? I'd really like to get some sleep.'

* * *

Sammy tried to kill all wayward thoughts, but her sleep was broken by them nonetheless. She awoke early the following morning to find that she was still thinking about him and the effect he had had on her.

She'd had a crush on him a million years ago. Was there a reluctant attraction still there? Some kind of hangover from back in the day when she had looked at him with her adolescent crush carefully hidden?

Beyond that, was there something about him, something compelling, that she still found vaguely irresistible? She'd made it her mission to be strong and independent—to turn her back on the path her mother had taken, when she'd collapsed after her husband had died and then had foolishly and weakly turned to a guy for support when she should have looked inwards for her own inner strength.

She'd carved her own niche, relied on her own resilience, and had always assumed that a guy would come in due course—someone decent and reliable who shared her dreams and would never let her down. Out there, there was paragon of virtue waiting for her.

So was she angry with herself because an attraction that belonged in the past had decided to resurface? Because she should feel nothing for a guy who was literally draped in red flags? And yet she did. It felt pathetic to tingle like a teenager when he'd touched her for no better reason than a performance.

When she looked at the Amazonian blonde, she could see the sort of woman he was attracted to. He was indifferent to *her* but it seemed she wasn't indifferent to *him*. She would have to start blotting out whatever foolish recollection of a crush had come along to ambush her common sense. She would have to match adult behaviour with adult behaviour.

She had a shower, dressed quickly in casual clothes and tentatively opened the bedroom door to see what awaited her outside. It was a little after seven and Rafael was at a desk by the window in front of his computer, working.

Every item of whatever he had used on the bed had been neatly tidied away and was folded on the coffee table in front of the television. Cushions were back in place. No one would guess that they had spent the night apart.

'I never saw you as a neat freak, Rafael.' She glanced at the folded clothes and then looked at him with her eyebrows raised.

'Isn't it great that you're discovering exciting, new stuff about the guy you're in love with?'

'Oh, yes, I can barely contain my excitement.'

'How did you sleep?'

'Terrific. Great bed; very comfortable. And you?'

'As well as can be expected on a sofa. Coffee?'

Rafael sat back and stretched, flexing his muscles, before standing up and strolling towards a coffee machine on a gleaming walnut sideboard which she only now noticed. The doors had been flung open to allow the balmy tropical air inside and, through them, she could glimpse a vista that could have been lifted straight from a magazine.

There was a distant view of bright-blue ocean, a stretch of greenery broken by swaying coconut trees—the very ones that surrounded the infinity pool—and bushes and foliage bursting with the bright colours of exotic flowers. All the familiar sounds were missing: the intrusive sounds of beeping horns, foot traffic outside her front door and the clatter of voices. It was peaceful and quiet, aside from birds, bees and the distant sound of a lawn mower doing something on the manicured grounds.

Determined not to let turbulent emotions get the better of her, Sammy smiled politely, nodded at his offer of coffee and strolled towards the open French doors.

He was barefoot in a loose white linen shirt and a pair of khaki shorts. He was so sinfully, spectacularly good-looking that it briefly took her breath away.

'It's okay to sit down, Sammy. We can go down in a while. No rush; breakfast is informal here. People grab what they want and at ten-thirty the day's work begins. We retire to one of the sitting rooms downstairs which is equipped with a conference table and all the gizmos to make transatlantic communication a breeze. Everybody else does whatever they want, although as I said today the partners will be on a day trip out and I'll take some time out to come with you to the market.'

'I'll see if I can get hold of some fresh fish and prawns. It wasn't the original plan for today, which was chicken, but …seafood would be nice.'

'There's an excellent fish market. Opens every day bar Monday.'

'When was the last time you were here, just out of curiosity?'

'Sorry?'

'When were you here last? I know it's not part of my brief to ask personal questions, but it might help if I know just a tiny bit about you, seeing as you're the love of my life.'

Their eyes met and Sammy held his dark gaze.

Rafael hesitated. He had got her to this place, and it made sense for them to have some background information about one another, but intense privacy was so embedded in his DNA that he honestly didn't know where to begin when it came to sharing anything about himself.

Her clear green eyes were only mildly curious.

She was so slight, and her dark hair was so short, that she should have looked boyish—but she didn't. She was all soft femininity underneath the tough, prickly exterior, a contradiction, and all the more unsettling and fascinating for it.

He poured them both a cup of coffee and nodded to the sofa, encouraging her to sit and then sitting next to her, inclining his body to face her and extending his long, muscular legs.

'Okay, you're right. I suppose it makes sense for us to find out a bit more about one another. I don't come here often, as it happens. Not as often as I'd like. Of course it gets used: my father comes on a reasonably regular basis, and brings friends sometimes. And I open it up to my employees on a regular basis—a kind of bonus if they've done a particularly good job. For me, though, time is money.'

'How did you get to that place?'

'Come again?'

'The place where time is money. I don't remember you being particularly impressed by money or material stuff when you were young. Old jeans…old rugby shirt… You always looked like you couldn't care less about fancy clothes.'

'I didn't then,' Rafael said gently, lowering his lashes. 'And I still don't, but I found that what I do care about—which is making the sort of money that gives me freedom—comes with the fancy clothes and the material stuff.'

'It's a tough life.'

Rafael burst out laughing and, when he looked at her, his dark eyes were warm and appreciative.

'Never thought about making lots of money, Sammy? Buying freedom from small-town living?'

'No,' she said politely. 'And frankly I'm shocked that, having met me, anyone out there is actually falling for this act of ours. Two minutes of questioning and they'd know what I thought of people who put money ahead of everything. I hope you don't think I'm rude in saying that.'

'Borderline rude, now that you mention it, but I'm getting used to that side of you.' His dark eyes were amused. 'I should point out, though, that I don't think anyone will be asking for your definition of what you look for in a soul mate. You're over-thinking conversations that won't take place. Between work, being a tour guide for the other halves and you buried in the kitchen, long, meaningful conversations are going to be few and far between. If the going gets tough, I'll rescue you.' He paused and then, to his surprise, said, 'Anyway, everyone cares about money.'

'Yes, well, maybe in your world.'

'Money is freedom. Who doesn't want to be free?' He reached for his phone and ordered up some breakfast, courtesy of one of the assistant chefs on call: local coconut bread with scrambled eggs and fresh juice. His eyes didn't leave her face. 'But, getting out of the realms of abstract thinking and returning to your original question, I've had the place for years. It was…'

'It was…?'

'A celebration of making my first million, as it happens.' He looked at her, but her returning gaze was bland and matter of fact. She was listening, but she wasn't hanging onto what he had to say. Something stirred inside him, something darkly tempting, a sensation that was as fleeting as quicksilver, gone before he could recognise it. Somewhere inside, a spark had been lit, and it left him with an uneasy feeling, one he dismissed as soon as it surfaced.

What was the big deal in sharing perfectly straightforward information because they happened to be in a situation that demanded it?

'My ancestry on my father's side harks from this island, as it happens. It was briefly colonised by the Spanish, hence the connection. My parents came here on a belated honeymoon when I was three.' He flushed darkly because *that* bit had slipped out before he could edit it.

'Okay, makes sense—I've read that it's tough buying land or property here without connections. How is your dad, by the way? I remember him…a bit.'

'Is that it? No more probing questions about my past in a quest for background information to add authenticity?'

'I can ask some if you like.' Sammy shrugged and then smiled. 'I thought we'd stick to the basics.'

'Excellent idea,' Rafael concurred a little tetchily. 'So, on the subject of the basics, my father is fine and living a splendid life in Valencia, which is where he comes from. After we left Yorkshire, he did a stint back in London, but then once I'd made my first million he expressed a desire to return to Spain after…after everything. It was well within my remit to give him what he wanted, so I did.'

'He must be very proud of you,' Sammy said thoughtfully. 'And honestly, Rafael, there's absolutely no need for you to come with me to get provisions. In fact, you'd be more of a hindrance than a help. I can dither a lot when it comes to buying fresh ingredients. I'll check out the kitchen before I go, and see what I need to prep and when, and if there's transport available…?'

'On tap.'

'Good.' She smiled briskly. 'If I'm to cook the meal I want to cook, then I'm going to have to leave very soon to go do my shopping.'

'No time? You're hurrying along the "getting to know me" business.'

'You enjoy. If I see anyone downstairs, I'll lay it on thick about the duties of a personal chef, and no time to waste. Between the roux and puff pastry, a girl could be tied up all day.'

Sammy leapt to her feet.

The market was an adventure. One of Rafael's dedicated drivers gave her a little tour around the town, pointing out where the various beaches were, telling her that she couldn't leave without visiting one of them. She had begun to feel two things for the first time in her life: on top of the world and in control.

They rolled down the windows and she let the breeze whip through her hair as she stared out at verdant roadside and bright-blue skies. Up ahead, telephone wires were covered in vines and ivy. The trees were bigger and lusher than any she'd ever seen before, and vegetation crowded the sides of the roads, as if in a hurry to stage a takeover. It was busy at ten in the morning with vans and scooters on the roads, and shops on the sides of the humming roads were open for business here and there with vivid fruit and vegetables spilling out from them.

They drove along the main road, zig-zagging, so that every now and then she would peer out and catch a glimpse of the ocean, which glittered a deeper blue than the sky and was as calm as a lake. Coconut trees were everywhere, springing up in unusual places, tangling with towering bamboo trees, the perfect playground for birds and butterflies.

Sammy was dropped in the square, on the fringe of the bustling market. Stepping out of the car, she took a few seconds to breathe in deeply, eyes half-closed, really loving the fragrant scent of flowers, sun and spices being sold, and enjoying the rich lilt of foreign voices that laughed and bartered.

She wasn't the only tourist enjoying the town although, thankfully, none of them were any of the women from the villa. The last thing she needed was to see a six-foot blonde swooping down on her.

She took her time shopping and let her mind drift from the food she was going to prepare to Rafael and some of the things he had let slip that had set the cogs in her brain whirring. She had a future that now seemed secure, a very happy trade-off for a few days of inconvenience.

Then she thought of the kiss that still lingered on her lips and was uneasily aware of the truth of the saying that there was no such thing as a free lunch. Would she face consequences of this decision that she couldn't foresee? Nope. She pushed that unease away, and was in high spirits by the time she made it back to the villa at a little after two, having grabbed something to eat at one of the local cafés.

The villa was quiet. Business was being done in one wing of the mansion and the partners were lazing on a beach somewhere, enjoying whatever five-star picnic had been prepared for them. Sammy got on with the business of preparing food with the radio on low, with the occasional sound of one of the housekeepers cleaning and a nice warm breeze rustling through the open doors.

Peace.

Sammy was most lost to the world when she was cooking. The kitchen was fragrant with the smells of herbs and spices and, before long, her bouillabaisse was done and dusted and absolutely perfect. She had got hold of three plump kingfish and was busy preparing them when she was aware of the soft pad of footsteps pausing at the door.

Victoria. She turned around with a sinking heart to see the other woman lounging against the door frame. Did the woman have *nothing* else to wear apart from items of clothing that could fit into matchboxes? The sarong draped loosely round her slim hips barely skimmed her thighs, and matched the pale-yellow shades of her bikini top. Her gold sandals were flat, but even so she towered over Sammy as she quietly shut the door behind her. She strolled to the centre of the kitchen before striking a dramatic pose as she half-perched on the ten-seater kitchen table. Her blonde hair was loose. It was very long, nearly to her waist, and hung attractively in damp strands over her shoulder.

'How was the beach?' Sammy eventually asked, because *someone* had to break the stretching silence, and Victoria seemed to have no interest in being the first to speak.

Sammy washed her hands and made an effort to smile, but was conscious of her food-splattered apron, lack of make-up and casual clothing that was great when behind a stove but less great when confronted by a woman whose job was to strut runways and dazzle.

'The beach was like any other beach.' Victoria shrugged one shoulder, but her bright-blue eyes were pinned to Sammy's flushed face with the coldness of diamonds. 'We really didn't get to know one another last night, did we?'

'It was a brief encounter,' Sammy agreed. 'Long-haul flying takes a toll.'

'Do you do much of that?'

'Very little. Is there something I can get for you? I ask because I'm in the middle of...' She made a vague expansive gesture towards the dishes still to be prepped and smiled ruefully without bothering to try to look sincere.

'Of course you are. A chef...fascinating. Rafael's managed to do a good job of keeping you under wraps! The last I heard, wasn't he dating that model who stole the Paris show a few months ago?'

'Was he? I wouldn't know. Not my world, I'm afraid.'

'I know! Adorable. So...remind me how you two met?'

'Perhaps another time, Victoria. I really would love nothing more than to sit and have a girlie chat about our relationship with you, but sadly I can't. So, if you don't mind...and I hate to be rude...?'

'Rafael never talked about his past when we were together. You *did* know that we were once very much *an item,* didn't you? Yes? So you can imagine my surprise when he produced you from the closet and told me that you were serious about one another!'

She wafted towards Sammy and stared down at her

from her imposing height. Having just returned from a day at the beach, she smelled of sun and sand without looking as though either had got the better of her.

'I've been naughty and done a little detective work, and, wow! Fabulous CV—and lucky you, living in that super-peaceful part of the world! Crazy that you and Rafael should end up together when he's just completely the opposite of you! I guess meeting up again after all those years… Memories, yeah? Powerful, amazing, *adorable*. Your mum lives up there in Yorkshire, doesn't she? I believe that's in the blurb I read about you. She must be thrilled that you two are together!'

'Over the moon. Now, please…'

'It's not going to last—you know that, don't you?'

'Because what *you* had with him didn't?' Sammy retorted through gritted teeth.

'Because *nothing lasts* with Rafe on the woman front. And face it—look at the women he's dated! If *they* couldn't tame him, if *I* couldn't, then do *you* really think you can?'

This temporarily rendered Sammy mute because she'd been thinking pretty much the same thing since she'd laid eyes on Victoria. Why would anyone seriously believe that the guy who went for statuesque blondes would ever suddenly be bowled over by a five-foot-three brunette with cropped hair? On the looks front alone, there was a glaring disparity there.

'So…' Victoria pouted, stepping back just as the door was pushed open behind them. 'I'm just being kind because I *care*.'

She was smiling as she turned to the kitchen door where Rafael was now standing, his posture mirroring Victoria's of only minutes before as he lounged against the door frame, his dark eyes cold and watchful.

'Looking for something, Victoria?'

'A bottle of water...'

She sashayed across the tiled floor, a picture of impossible physical perfection, and paused next to Rafael just close enough and long enough for Sammy to get the picture that *she* was what a guy like Rafael Moreno would always and inevitably be attracted to.

'But...' she laughed huskily and glanced over her shoulder at Sammy '...then I remembered that there are bottles in the mini-fridge in the bedroom.'

Rafael watched her march past him, then looked back at Sammy. 'What was that all about?' He moved towards her as she was turning away and spun her gently round so that she had no option but to look at him.

'Nothing.'

'Sammy, I can see that you're upset.'

'I can handle something like that. I can handle *some-one* like that. You try working as a sous chef! You'd soon find out that it pays to be as tough as nails.'

'Why am I not convinced?'

'Because...because...'

'What did she say to you? If she's put a foot out of place, trust me, I won't hesitate to remind her of the mistake.'

'You don't need to defend me!' But her voice was a whisper and tears weren't too far away. Why—because she'd been taken down a peg or two? Made to see just how unsuitable she was for a guy like Rafael? *Because she'd been put in her place? Pathetic.* She'd surely been through enough not to let someone like Victoria get to her?

'You're my better half—at least for a week.' He pulled her gently towards him and as Sammy rested her head against his chest, she could hear the crooked smile in his voice.

'That doesn't count.'

'Ignore her, Sammy. You're a million times more of a woman than she could ever be.'

Sammy tilted her head to look at him. She had to crane her neck. 'That's not what the mirror's saying. Rafael, she just pointed out the obvious—why would a guy like you be attracted to someone like me? She just reminded me of how beautiful she was and how ordinary I am in comparison.' Self-pity clogged her throat. *Crazy. Stupid.*

'If you think you're ordinary, Sammy, then maybe you and the mirror need to get to know one another better. You're cute and feisty and sexy as hell, and truth is, I don't think I've ever met any woman quite like you.'

Sammy's mouth fell open.

Their eyes collided and in that split second she knew what Rafael was going to do. He was going to kiss her—a *real* kiss, with no audience in need of convincing.

Never had she wanted anything more badly in her life.

She gasped as his mouth descended, as his tongue plunged into the moistness of her mouth. She arched up to him, her body contouring his, slight and small against big and muscular.

She moaned in a hitched way as he swept her off her feet, their mouths still devouring one another's, and rested her on the table. He supported himself, hands flattened against the smooth, cool concrete surface of the table, and she wrapped her arms around his neck and didn't surface for air until the kiss slowed.

They were breathing heavily as they broke apart.

'Well…' Sammy broke the silence but then stuttered to a stop because she had no idea what to say, nor why her fingers were still sifting through his hair.

'Well.' Rafael smiled slowly. His hands on the table were still caging her but then he raised one to delicately trail a finger along her cheek. 'What are we going to do about this?'

'Nothing,' Sammy said quickly. 'We… I… This shouldn't have happened. We can just forget about it and carry on as though…as though…' She yanked her disobedient hand away and sat on it.

'Or…?'

'Rafael, don't…'

'Up to you,' he murmured, contouring her mouth in a sinfully erotic gesture. 'I'll sleep on the sofa until you command me to join you in bed. A gentleman couldn't say fairer than that, could he?'

That damned smile! That unfair way he roused her, so that her nipples pinched and the wetness between her legs made her want to fidget and squirm!

She didn't want the complication of this attraction! She *appreciated* that he was being a gentleman. She just wasn't sure that a gentleman was what she wanted…

CHAPTER SIX

OUT OF THE corner of his eye, Rafael was aware of Victoria holding court with a couple of the partners. The partners looked a little alarmed. In a minute, he would think about rescuing them, because Victoria had obviously had a little too much to drink and the canapés had not even made their appearance. By the time dinner was served, who knew where she would be on the inebriation scale?

Clement was saying something about business and Rafael dragged his thoughts back in line. It was a little before seven and they were all milling around in the sitting room, which was spacious and kitted out with an assortment of chairs and sofas all in shades of creams and pale-gold. Everything was artfully arranged so that no one would be left out of any group conversations. Unless anyone wanted to lurk in a corner, they were compelled to sit in a sociable arrangement and chat. Excellent for fostering a cordial atmosphere amongst people who might not know one another that well. Staff had been hired for the week and champagne flutes were being refilled.

Clement had turned to Geoffrey, a dapper middle-aged guy who was desperate for his small company to be amalgamated under a bigger umbrella so that their software could expand. Clement was musing about the stock market and what might prove a good investment. Rafael wondered if he was aware of his girlfriend over-gesticulating in the background. It didn't seem so. He was a talented businessman whose ability to focus was legendary. Victoria could have been doing cartwheels on the ceiling.

Rafael glanced at his watch and drained his glass—whisky, not champagne.

Where was Sammy?

She'd disappeared to the market first thing and since then he had only clapped eyes on her once, in the kitchen, where she'd been surrounded by mountains of fresh fruit and vegetables, and had shooed him out before he'd had a chance to remind her that she had to make an appearance in time for drinks.

Hell, was she even thinking of that kiss they'd shared? Because he couldn't get it out of his mind. He could still taste it on his mouth!

Let the two sous chefs he had hired get on with the nitty-gritty, he had told her. They needed the practice before they took up their positions at his hotel, and he and Sammy had to keep up their charade.

'I'll be there, don't worry.' She had pushed him firmly in the direction of the door. 'I haven't forgotten our deal!'

He breathed in deeply and remembered those big, green eyes staring up at him with amusement, and those soft lips that had done too good a job of reminding him what they'd felt like against his.

Rafael wasn't sure whether it was the novelty of their situation or the fact that there was history between them, but he was drawn to Sammy in a way that was confusing and a little unsettling. Where did that pull come from which made his mind wander off in the middle of back-to-back meetings; and which made him lose concentration until the only thing he could think of was seeing what she was up to? It had driven him to seek her out in the kitchen…because he just couldn't put that kiss to the back of his mind.

He wondered whether maybe the stark contrast between Victoria and Sammy was somehow messing with his head even though it shouldn't have, of course, because Victoria was an ex and Sammy was… Sammy wasn't even *current* in the truest sense of the word.

Victoria was a reminder of his greatest screw-up when it came to any relationship he had ever had with a woman. He hadn't so much as taken his eye off the ball as never had his eye on it in the first place. In the dying throes of their relationship, clinging and sobbing had alternated with threats of revenge, followed swiftly by tearful apologies and yet more clinging. It had been a mess.

Was his mind doing some kind of foxtrot between what Victoria represented and what Sammy represented, coerced into a phony relationship? Whereas Victoria had been an uncontrolled mess, Sammy couldn't be more controlled. She was as cool as a cucumber. She had no idea how those passing, dutiful touches had turned him on the evening before, whether he liked to admit it or not. She was playing a game for his benefit, and only because the carrot he had dangled in front of her had been too tempting to resist.

For the first time in his life, he was with a woman who wasn't chasing behind him and wasn't after more than he was willing to give. She didn't want to hear his back story so that she could get closer. In fact, she wasn't that interested in his back story at all. Their paths had crossed briefly when they'd been teenagers, and the experience had left a sour taste in her mouth. Left to her own devices, there was no way she would ever have sought him out because she just didn't like him very much. She wasn't impressed by his money, even though it was thanks to his millions that she was being given a passport to everything she had ever wanted for herself.

Although, he grudgingly had to admit, it was also thanks to his money that she'd lost the space she'd banked on having for herself in the first place—swings and roundabouts.

Whatever was going on, he was still trying to make sense of it. Victoria and Sammy side by side... Was Sammy somehow benefiting from the comparison— was that it? He was always in control when it came to women, so what was happening here? It was puzzling but it was also...exciting...even though he knew that this kind of excitement wasn't something he should be indulging.

His last brief fling had ended four months ago, with a striking model who had told him that he needed to grow up—by which she'd meant start committing to more than whatever lay a day or two ahead. He'd politely turned down the suggestion.

Maybe he was sick of models and was now vulnerable to falling for a feisty, down-to-earth girl from his past who didn't think twice about laughing at him and couldn't care less about commitment—at least, not with him. Was that it? He felt that, if he couldn't make sense of what he was feeling, he couldn't control it, which obviously wouldn't do.

He was in the process of trying to juggle his thoughts with whatever conversation was going on with the two guys standing by him when he glanced towards the door and...there she was.

For a few seconds, all the background noise faded and Rafael drew in a sharp breath as he stared at her over the rim of his glass with dark, brooding intensity. Every muscle in his body had tightened and the thud of a powerful sexual awareness hit him like a sledgehammer.

She was wearing the simplest of summer dresses, something straight and flowery, with tiny pearl buttons all the way down the front and thin spaghetti straps. She wore flat sandals, no jewellery except for some stud earrings and next to no make-up. She looked young, fresh, wholesome and incredibly sexy.

He cleared his throat and managed to propel himself towards her, dumping his empty glass en route and grabbing a replacement in the process.

'Sammy, my darling, you're here.' He managed to sound hearty yet caressingly intimate at the same time.

* * *

'Rafael, my love. Where else would I be?'

Sammy felt her heart pick up speed. She'd almost completely managed to avoid him during the course of the day. First, she'd been at the market, and then later she'd made sure that one of her young helpers, Jemima, had done the honours serving a casual picnic lunch at the pool house where the workers had been taking a break to eat.

He'd shown up at the kitchen at some point, purely to chat to her about her duties. She'd glanced at him leaning indolently against the door frame and had gone hot and cold with sudden, dramatic awareness. God knew, she'd tried to put that kiss they'd shared into perspective, but she hadn't been able to. It had detonated like a hand grenade tossed into her calm, ordered life.

She didn't get it. How could he manage to get under her skin the way he did? He shouldn't be able to bring a smile to her lips, and he certainly shouldn't be able to ratchet up her curiosity about him until her head ached, but he did both. She'd kept telling herself that this was just a job, and that just about seemed to work until she laid eyes on him.

Such as now. He was in black: black jeans and a black figure-hugging tee-shirt, tan loafers and no socks. Nothing about him screamed 'wealth' and yet he still managed to look incredibly rich, laid back and sophisticated. Just behind him, she caught a glimpse of Victoria narrowly watching their interaction with a champagne flute half-raised, as though she'd been on the verge of gulping down the contents.

'You didn't expect me to still be shackled to the oven, did you?' she purred, conscious of Victoria's eyes on them. She was also aware of *his* eyes on her, a little amused and a little surprised. He'd obviously thought that getting her to pretend to respond to him convincingly would be as difficult as pulling teeth.

She looked up at him, placed her hand flat on his chest and stood on tiptoe, half-closing her eyes, mouth pursed for the kiss everyone would be expecting—something light and brief, in keeping with the fact that he wasn't the touchy-feely sort and public displays of affection weren't really his thing.

His mouth was cool and she started as he nudged his tongue between her lips, teasing a response from her and getting just the response she knew she definitely shouldn't give. Her hand curled into a fist, clasping the soft cotton of his tee-shirt. Her eyelids fluttered as she unconsciously gravitated towards him until their bodies were pressed together.

Sammy was drowning in that kiss. Her breathing slowed and, when he eventually made to pull away, she found that she was trembling.

'Now, *there's* a surprise,' he murmured softly into her ear.

She cupped the side of his cheek with her hand, still on tiptoe to reach him, but pulling him down slightly so that, as softly as he'd whispered into her ear, she could whisper back, 'Why? I do know the rules of the game,

Rafael. Besides, your ex is all eyes. You don't want her to start getting suspicious, do you? I thought that was the whole point of the game.'

'So it is, my darling, so it is.'

Sammy pulled back, tore her gaze away from his and then peered around him to the assembled crowd. She smiled.

'Young love!' One of the older women raised her champagne flute with a broad, approving smile. Sammy laughed and pretend-punched Rafael in the stomach. She said something about maybe young love for *her,* but slightly less young for Rafael, who was a few years older.

She avoided Victoria. She mingled and chatted but was doubly aware of the other woman's shrewd eyes on her, and of Rafael always nearby, probably making sure she didn't put her foot in it somehow by saying the wrong thing.

He gently tugged her back as everyone began making their way to the dining room where dinner was being served. Ahead of them, Victoria had fallen into step with Clement. His arm was around her waist but he was talking to one of the other men. If he was even aware of the towering blonde at his side, then he gave very little evidence of it.

'Just look at that,' Sammy muttered to Rafael as they trailed behind them.

'Look at what?'

'Victoria and Clement.'

'What about them?'

'He's barely paying her a scrap of attention.'

'Not sure what you'd like him to be doing right now. He's pushing eighty. I don't think hijinks on the dance floor are going to work for him.'

Sammy glanced up to find Rafael grinning broadly. He looked down at her. Their eyes met and her heart sped up.

'Why on earth would he go out with her if he wasn't interested in her?'

'Of course he's interested in her, although, in fairness, possibly not for her mind.'

'He's a really nice guy, but I suppose when you've got tons of money, and you can have whatever toy you want, you're always going to pick the one that's the shiniest.'

'He *is* getting over his wife's death,' Rafael said gently. 'Maybe the shiniest toy in the toy box is just what he needs for his recovery. Besides, it's a symbiotic relationship.'

'Meaning?'

'Victoria likes his money and he likes being seen with her on his arm.'

'Rich men—they're all the same.'

'Tut-tut, Sammy. That sounds a lot like a generalisation.'

'Does it?' She stopped dead in her tracks and looked at him. 'I'm thinking that *your* track record is along those lines!—beautiful women hanging onto you and you having fun with them even though you're not in it for their minds? Honestly, I just don't get women sometimes.'

Rafael was still grinning. 'You're very fetching when

you're standing on your soap box. Has anyone ever told you that?'

'Actually, no.' But she could feel herself tumbling into his dark gaze. She drew in a sharp breath when he raised one finger to trail it along her cheek, finally outlining her mouth and letting his finger linger there for a few seconds. Her eyes widened and everything in her body suddenly began to disobey the rules. Her nipples tightened against the thin cotton of her dress. She was so flat that she could easily do without a bra, and she wasn't wearing one now. A spreading dampness between her legs made her want to rub them together. Her pulse was racing.

'There's no need for that,' she managed to say breathlessly as his finger continued to linger on her face.

'Oh, yes,' Rafael apologised in a voice that sounded far from apologetic. 'I didn't realise that there's just two of us here. Everyone else has made it to the dining room. We'd better race there or else they'll be wondering where we are—maybe thinking that the love birds decided to dump the dinner and just do the sex.'

'Don't say that!'

'Just a little joke, Sammy. No need to get ruffled about it. You're as red as a beetroot.'

'Yes, well, it pays to remember that this is…is *a charade*. It's not real! We just do…that kind of stuff when other people are around.'

Rafael had obediently lowered his hand but there was coolness where his finger had been and Sammy hated herself for wishing that it was still caressing her cheek and setting her body aflame in the process.

Dump the dinner and just do the sex...

The throwaway remark sent her imagination whirling into frantic overdrive. She spun round on her heels and began walking briskly towards the dining room.

She just *knew* that he was still grinning as he followed her. Could the man see what was going through her head? Did he know the effect he had on her with those casual, meaningless touches?

She sincerely hoped not. Sammy knew the kind of guy he was. He was a rich man who snapped his fingers and had any woman he wanted come running at speed to do his bidding until he got bored with them. He would call that a generalisation but there was more than just a grain of truth in it—more than several *thousand* grains of truth in it. The last thing she wanted was for him to think that she was anything like all those other women—floored by his charm, bewitched by his wit and intelligence and turned on by his stupid good looks.

She forced herself to remember him as a teenager, bunking off school and leading her brother astray—much safer. But as they hit the dining room, which was abuzz with everyone peering at the seating plan, laughing and chatting, he caught up with her. She felt the weight of his arm around her waist as he pulled her back against him and lowered his head to breathe in her newly washed hair.

'This is one of those times, Sammy,' he murmured, and she twisted so that she was looking up at him with a puzzled frown.

'One of *what* times?'

'I can't have my beautiful partner looking as though

we've just had an argument. We need to be married at least a year for that. So, my darling…' He kissed her softly, sweetly and briefly, and that soft, sweet, brief kiss knocked her senseless.

Her head was all over the place as they drew apart but it was ages before she could really focus on what was going on around her: the praise for the food she'd made; the questions about the market and what the fresh produce had been like; her plans for the place she wanted to open when she and Rafael returned to England. The champagne continued to flow, and she knew that she was smiling and chatting and answering questions, but all she could think of was Rafael: the way he made her feel and the stupidity of *feeling* the way he made her feel.

She even forgot about Victoria, though her not-so-dulcet tones seemed to dominate whatever conversation was happening at the other end of the long, rectangular table.

Between courses, Sammy excused herself so that she could supervise the next array of dishes to be served. She'd had just two glasses of champagne, and her head was in a very sober place when she re-entered the dining room to announce her dessert, only to be pre-empted by Victoria; she had gone from tipsy to word-slurring over the course of the evening.

Sammy shot Rafael a panicked glance as the towering blonde rose unsteadily to her feet and tapped her spoon on her champagne flute until everyone fell into bemused silence.

He gestured to Sammy to come and take her empty

seat, and Sammy duly went to sit next to him. She was immediately reassured by the mere fact of him sitting next to her. Something about the warmth and rock-solid self-assurance he emanated made her feel as though, whatever happened, he would be able to sort it out.

Desserts were now being served as the room waited for Victoria to speak with Jemima and another assistant, Trisha, placing delicate bowls of tropical fruit salad and soursop ice-cream in front of everyone.

Victoria looked around imperiously, swaying slightly. Next to her, Clement was frowning with a hint of disapproving impatience.

'What's going on, Rafael?' Sammy snapped under her breath.

'I feel this is a "wait and see" situation,' he murmured in return but then he clasped her hand under the table, resting it on his thigh. Sammy felt herself relax just a little.

'To the love birds!' Victoria pinned her eyes on them and raised her glass. Everyone else duly raised theirs too and Sammy decided that she could deal with a drunken toast to love birds.

'Who would have thought? What a shock for the man who lives in the gossip columns to have finally found true love, and so *quickly*!'

Sammy's smile froze and her fingers curled a little more tightly with Rafael's.

'I just hope it's the real deal!' Victoria waggled her finger in a reproving manner while everyone began to look just a tiny bit uncomfortable. 'Because this is one very special lady!'

'That's enough, Victoria.' Clement's voice was mild but sufficiently commanding for her to hesitate and glance down at him.

'I just want to wish the happy couple my congratulations!' Victoria pouted. She stroked Clement's head and swigged some champagne for good measure. Then she looked back at them and flashed her eyes with teasing intent. 'So, can you tell us if we all need to start looking for wedding hats...?'

Sammy froze. She felt Rafael tense next to her. He rose to his feet, coolly thanked Victoria for her good wishes and then looked at Clement. 'I think,' he murmured, 'that girlfriend of yours needs to get some beauty sleep just as soon as dessert is done and dusted. A little too much champagne can sometimes be a very bad idea.'

It wrapped up the moment of awkwardness, but twenty minutes later, with everyone tired and yawning and the conversation back to less fraught topics, Clement paused by Rafael. He looked at him, then at Sammy, with a smile.

'Well, my boy.' He leant towards them, his eyes sharp and as bright as a sparrow's. 'You've found yourself a good one here.'

Sammy blushed. Her gut feeling was that Rafael might perhaps disagree with that statement, considering they'd only been thrown into this situation by a series of unfortunate events.

'Victoria may have had a little too much of the fine

stuff for her own good, but she was spot-on when she said that this is a very special lady.' He tapped the side of his nose and smiled. 'Love at first sight—although it's not quite that in your case—is certainly to be recommended. My Gail and I fell in love and within minutes I knew that I was going to marry her.'

His voice was wistful. 'I thoroughly approve. So, if a proposal is on the cards, then you truly have my congratulations. It certainly is a fine thought to know that the company my dear wife and I built together will be under the auspices of a family man whose heart is in the right place.'

He straightened and nodded to Victoria, who was fidgeting in the background. She followed him out of the room along with everyone else, leaving Sammy and Rafael in the dining room on their own.

Rafael rose and immediately went to a sideboard and helped himself to some whisky, grabbing a glass of wine for Sammy. He shut the door to the dining room and slanted a glance at the remains of the day: plates, glasses and yet more glasses and bottles, all to be cleared later. Right now, he was busy wondering what the hell had just happened.

'So...' He sat, manoeuvring his chair so that he was facing her and leaned his long legs to one side.

'So...' Sammy parroted dubiously.

'Victoria was just mischief-making.'

'She implied that we were about to get married. We've

gone from being an item to being practically engaged. I'm not sure I'm that comfortable with that.'

'Why? One remark about wedding hats from someone who'd had too much to drink does not an impending marriage make.'

'Why? *Why?* Engagements and weddings are serious business! At least, they are to people like me who live in the real world.'

'My world's very real.'

Sammy swept aside that interruption and fixed him with a baleful stare. 'Plus, poor Clement seems to now think that wedding rings are going to be exchanged.'

'Yes, that's a little unfortunate,' Rafael admitted. 'He may have gone off the rails with Victoria in an attempt to distract himself from his grief, but he's always been a family guy, and the fact that he now assumes that I'm a reformed character might ease any lingering doubts he might have about this deal.'

'Is that likely? I thought it was all but done and dusted.'

'To quote that well-worn saying, "there's many a slip twixt cup and lip"… I wouldn't want him to start suspecting that there's anything fishy going on.' He raised his eyebrows. 'You shouldn't have been so charming.'

Rafael sipped his drink and looked at her. She was blushing. He'd never met any woman who blushed as much as she did, but then, she had none of the hard edges of the women he dated. She was basically a country girl with wide-eyed dreams who believed in love and romance. As she'd just said, engagements and weddings were a serious business. She'd been his fake girlfriend and now practically his fake fiancée—at least while they were out here—and he definitely shouldn't look at her the way he was doing now. He lowered his eyes even though he could still see her image printed on his retina.

'Nothing changes,' he said gruffly. 'Victoria knows where her bread is temporarily buttered and, as you can see, she may tower over Clement but he's still the guy in charge.'

'It just feels as though we're on a slippery slope...'

'Same slope, different wording. 'Fiancée' implies commitment, a bond that goes beyond two people in it for a bit of fun. We could start launching into disclaimer speeches but my feeling is that that would just end up muddying the waters. This deal is hugely important and not just to me. The ripples of its outcome will be felt by many. There's nothing to worry about—after all, what's a fiancée but a partner with a ring on her finger?'

Even so, Rafael agreed with her. It *did* feel as though they were on a slippery slope, but what confused him was that the slippery slope wasn't the result of this small complication. An inebriated, vengeful ex-girlfriend could say what she liked. Neither he nor Sammy had admitted anything about heading down the aisle any time soon, and if anyone else mentioned that at any point he knew that he could always laugh it off.

No, the slippery slope was what was happening inside him: the wild excitement he was getting from Sammy playing the part of his devoted girlfriend; the sneaky enjoyment he got from the blurring of those lines between reality and fantasy. It surprised him, but when he thought about it stopping some crazy desire in him refused to see common sense.

Even now, discussing Victoria and her malicious interjection with no one around to witness anything, he still wanted to reach out and brush his hand against her cheek to feel the cool smoothness of her skin against his palm.

He balled his fists and gulped down some whisky.

Sammy didn't seem to notice his turmoil; in fact, she seemed to be deep in thought. 'You're right,' she said eventually.

'So we're good?' Rafael asked, snapping back to the present.

'It's just a week.'

'I could have a quiet word with Clement as a precaution…mention that we're both very private people who would rather our relationship remain private before any official announcements are made.'

'What about everyone else?'

'I very much doubt any of them has any interest in broadcasting anything. Victoria is the loose cannon but if Clement passes on my words of caution, then have no fear, she'll listen to him.'

Strip away any media coverage a vindictive ex might spread, pretend that was never going to happen, and things still seemed to have shifted. The game felt a whole lot more serious now. The physical contact…the urge to touch… It felt as though there might be quicksand under his feet…

'What do you see in them, Rafael?'

'Come again?'

'Victoria…all those models you go out with…what do you see in them? I mean, Victoria might have been a little screwed up and got hold of the wrong end of the stick with you, but those are the sort of women you date, aren't they? Models—a rich man with no other wish than to have a shiny bauble on his arm, like Clement. Although, I feel that Clement will soon tire of his shiny bauble because he knows what it's like to have the real deal at his side. But you, Rafael… I just don't get it.'

Rafael shook his head in a cobweb-clearing kind of way, but her eyes remained steady when he finally looked at her.

'You don't have to answer that,' she said abruptly. 'This is a pretend relationship, and in pretend relationships two people don't have to do anything but pretend to be attracted to one another and pretend to know each other's history.'

She began rising to her feet and he impulsively reached out to stay her. Why? He was as surprised by the gesture as she seemed to be, although she slowly sat back down and stared at him. Those amazing eyes, he thought distractedly. How could green, calm, slightly curious eyes be so distracting?

'It's complicated,' he heard himself mutter.

'Life's complicated,' Sammy returned. 'Look at where the pair of us are right now! Two people who couldn't be at further ends of the pole when it comes to…just about everything.' She paused. 'What's complicated?'

'I didn't want to end up like my dad.'

'What on earth do you mean?'

'He sold his soul to a woman and that woman took him for a ride. The woman was my mother. When my dad and I moved to your part of the world, I was in a pretty rough place. My mother had dumped the marriage in favour of a guy with a lot more money and my father fell apart at the seams—as if someone had pulled a vital piece of thread that had made the whole shoddy garment unravel. I picked up the pieces, and realised that it was no good handing over your soul to any woman, because the end of that road might not be what you had in mind. So, yes, I date models because I like knowing what I'm getting into. I enjoy the fact that they like my money. I can handle that.'

'Your poor dad. I wish I'd known him a little better. He always seemed so polite and quiet.'

'He was a broken man. I prefer to go through life in one piece. Don't get me wrong—I love my father very much—but that never made me blind to his faults.'

'He was just someone who trusted,' Sammy said gently. 'Which isn't a crime. What's love but a leap of faith?'

'Which,' Rafael drawled, rising to his feet and shoving his hands in the pockets of his black jeans, 'makes me realise just how perfect this arrangement between us is. No leap of faith, and we both know exactly where we stand.'

Sammy smiled back at him and stood up, brushing away some non-existent crumbs from her dress.

'I should stay down here for a bit and supervise what

to do with the leftover food. I don't want anything to go to waste.'

Rafael nodded. 'Up to you,' he said gruffly. He raked his fingers through his hair and shifted. Yes, she should stay down here…but he didn't want her to. He wanted her right by him, near him. Was he feeding this attraction? It was a disturbing thought and one he wanted to dismiss straight away. Boundaries were needed, and distance—none of this unholy want that overtook all his common sense.

'Yes, it is. So, I'll be up when I'm up, and Rafael…? You're right. Nothing to see here, as far as Victoria and her mischief-making goes, but it would be a good idea to say something to Clement just in case. And as for this *thing* between us, this arrangement? It works well because we know the boundary lines between us and there are no leaps of faith to be made.'

She laughed. 'I would say, as *understandings* go, as a win-win situation, it couldn't be more perfect.'

CHAPTER SEVEN

DID SHE KNOW exactly where they stood? She should do. She and Rafael were business associates who had temporarily joined forces to conclude a deal that would be beneficial to both of them. That was what she thought every time he wasn't around. It was a very reassuring approach to the situation.

For the past three days, ever since he had reinstalled those boundary lines between them, Sammy had done her best to take refuge in the kitchen. So long as she was there, hiding away with her two assistants behind pots, pans, hobs and ovens, she could just about manage to get her brain to do its thing and sternly repeat the mantra about them just being business associates.

Unfortunately, the minute she was in his presence, the last thing she felt like was a business associate. He was just sticking to the brief, playing the perfect partner, sending her hot sidelong glances when eyes were on them, and holding her lightly but intimately in a way that conformed to the image of the possessive guy who just couldn't keep his hands off his woman.

And, however cool and composed she tried to be, her body went up in flames at the slightest touch. The key thing was to make sure he didn't see the effect he had on her, but it was hard, because she had to respond in kind, which only turned whatever fire she was trying to control into a full-blown combustion.

The evening before, he had dipped a kiss on the side of her neck, a perfunctory piece of terrific acting, and she'd wanted to pass out. So for the past two nights she'd lurked in the kitchen until everyone had headed up, taking her time prepping for meals the following day and doing all sorts of unnecessarily complicated recipes that required far more attention than the end result probably warranted. And it had worked because, by the time she'd headed up to their suite, he'd been at the desk working and she'd been way too tired to do anything but yawn and then vanish into the safety of her bedroom. And she was up with the larks in the morning to finish the dishes she had spent the night before prepping.

They only really went into their acting roles at dinner but, even so, Sammy knew that she was going to be a wreck by the time the end of the week arrived.

On the bright side, however, whatever chat Rafael had had with Clement had succeeded because Victoria had backed off. If Sammy could have kept a level head, things would have been easier. Actually, if she could have stuck to the routine she had established—fragile though the routine was, because he could still manage to get to her with a sidelong look or a hint of a smile—she could just about have managed.

But tonight…no cooking. She had a night off.

Sammy stared at her reflection in the full-length mirror in the bedroom. It was a little after six-thirty. She had the windows open and she could hear the orchestra of music from all the insects, frogs and toads in the tropical foliage outside. She could also hear the sound of voices and laughter, because everyone was by the pool, gathering for a night on the town.

'I should really hang back,' she had said to Rafael the day before when the plan had been announced. 'Food to prep...'

'There's no dinner to prepare.'

'Lunch.'

'The other halves will be out again, exploring one of the more remote beaches. They'll be very happy with some local fare. I've made sure that my driver has sorted that out.'

'Yes but...'

'You're fishing for excuses not to come,' he had said irritably, his dark eyes cool. 'And it's not going to work. You clearly don't like this situation any more than I do, but we both signed up to it, so you're just going to have to factor in a night of relaxation.'

That sudden coolness in his voice had been a stark reminder of just how detached he was from the effects of the game they were playing. While she was a bag of nerves, he was as cool as a cucumber. He could kiss her and look at her with such heat that she could feel herself burning up, but none of it was real, and it was a real headache trying to deal with that.

'And this is a club,' he'd added for good measure.

'There'll be dancing and drinking so feel free to wear…
whatever sexy little number you've brought with you.'

He'd grinned then, all coldness gone, and she'd wondered whether he was teasing her. Did he think that she
was as wholesome as apple pie so couldn't possibly dress
like…all those other women he was accustomed to dating?

Still, staring at her reflection now, Sammy thought
about the outfits Victoria had showed up in for the past
few nights: small and tight and leaving very little to the
imagination. She was eye candy on a major scale. All the
other women, who were much older, dressed expensively
and sensibly: cotton and silk in neutral shades; elegant
and timeless. Sammy had pictured the much younger ver-
sions of them dressed in exactly the same way—pearls
and diamonds, nothing too short and nothing too tight;
nothing tasteless.

Just the sort that Rafael would never be drawn to in a
million years. She wondered whether Victoria secretly
sneered at her. Of course, that didn't matter, but still…
Summer sundresses and flat shoes worked well enough;
and of course loose, workmanlike clothes worked for the
kitchen because comfort was everything. But in a revela-
tory flash she'd seen herself from the outside and hadn't
been overjoyed with the image.

So tonight…something different. Having brought
nothing *sexy* with her to wear—not that she actually
owned anything that could be called sexy—Sammy had
sneaked in a couple of hours shopping on her own while
everyone had been occupied, the partners hiding under

hats on whatever beach they'd gone to, their other halves poring over documents ready for signing off.

She'd had fun. Shopping wasn't usually her thing, but this was different because she was shopping for a reason: to shock. Nothing too dramatic, because she wasn't dramatic by nature, but she wanted to assert herself as someone other than the hard-working, talented chef Rafael had been drawn to in some unlikely turn of events.

Now she slipped on her shoes, took a deep breath and headed downstairs to the join the party. Several cars were laid on for all of them and, if she hadn't got her skates on, Rafael would have been up in a minute, knocking on the bedroom door and asking whether she'd decided to find some other half-baked excuse for getting out of the evening.

Rafael glanced at his watch.

He always seemed to be glancing at his watch when it came to 'the love of his life'. It had occurred to him only the evening before that no woman had ever kept him waiting as much as this particular one did.

And, sure enough, he was waiting now. She should have been here fifteen minutes ago. He could see Victoria surreptitiously looking at him out of the corner of her eye.

Thank God he'd had a word with with Clement and her—a gentle reminder to Clement that Victoria might want to take a more subdued approach to his very private relationship with Sammy.

'We're both very private people,' he had confided,

whilst wondering how he had got to the point where this felt so much more dangerous than the harmless game of make-believe they had initiated a million years ago. 'The last thing either of us want or need is for our…er…situation to be discussed on an hourly basis.'

To Victoria, he had simply said, 'Any more toasts to the happy couple, and I'll make sure that Clement knows just how unwelcome we both find the attention. You wouldn't want him to disappoint him, would you?'

He hadn't bothered to explain why he didn't want the attention. He didn't bother to paper over the fact that she might have been a little perplexed at this from a guy who had never cared about anyone having an opinion on the love interests he had never sought to hide from public view. He knew that his peculiar change of stance would denote the seriousness of his relationship with Sammy.

He knew how Victoria's mind worked. The very fact that he wanted privacy would signify the importance of the relationship. Add to that the fact that he'd gone for a woman so completely different from any other woman he'd ever been involved with.

Deep in his thoughts, it took him a couple of seconds to register Sammy's arrival. Or maybe he'd just not been expecting the woman standing framed in the sliding panels of glass that led out to the back gardens. The lights from behind silhouetted her slender frame, the slim arms, the next-to-nothing waist, the delicate column of her neck and the short, short hair that emphasised the elfin prettiness of her face.

She was in some kind of wraparound sarong. It was

gossamer-flimsy and fell to mid-thigh in a riot of orange, russet and blue. The vest top she was wearing revealed the small roundness of her breasts and the toned slenderness of her arms. The practical sandals, which had been a staple of her wardrobe for the past few days, had been replaced by some silver sandals with thin straps that criss-crossed her ankles in a vaguely gladiatrix style.

One hand was on her hip, the other holding a little bag that matched the sandals. Very, very slowly Rafael began walking towards her. She didn't move a muscle as he approached.

'You...' He raked his fingers through his hair when he was finally standing in front of her. 'You...you've dressed for the occasion.'

'I thought I would.'

'Good. Good.'

He was struggling to recapture his self-control. He reminded himself, as he had reminded her only a couple of days ago, that their relationship was nothing more than a business arrangement. He'd got caught up in a lapse of concentration at the time and had told her about his father, about the problems he had faced as a teenager when she'd known him all those years ago.

Of course, he'd immediately regretted confiding in her and had made sure to swiftly remind her that any momentary sharing of personal information wasn't a gateway to...to *anything*...just in case she'd got it into her head that it might be. As it turned out, he shouldn't have bothered, because she hadn't mentioned a word about it since. In fact, she had reverted to type, only showing up on a need-to-show-up basis.

Such as now, dressed in something soft, small and revealing. His eyes dipped and he sucked in his breath at the realisation that she wasn't wearing a bra.

'Are you okay?'

'What's that?' Rafael belatedly pulled himself together, but he could feel the thrust of an erection bulging against his grey linen trousers and he had to look away fast. ''Course I'm okay,' he ground out. 'I was just... I suppose...wondering whether you were going to show up.'

'I told you that I would. Isn't this the part where we should be falling into one another's arms so that we can convince everyone that this is the real thing?' She shot him a disarming, coy smile.

He was floored. Where was the blushing girl he had grown accustomed to over the past few days?

She reached up and ran her hand gently along his neck, curving the strong jaw, which he clenched in response.

'What are you doing?' he demanded huskily.

'I'm playing to the audience. Isn't that what we're supposed to do?' She made a show of peering around him slightly. 'I can actually see the malevolent ex glaring in our direction.'

'Sammy...'

'Yes?'

'What you're doing isn't so much playing to the audience as playing with fire.'

* * *

Sammy could feel her heart picking up speed. She could see from the look on Rafael's face that she had shocked him with her outfit.

How on earth could something as superficial as an *outfit* shock a guy like him? And yet, as he had walked towards her, she had seen the darkening in his eyes. He was taking her in, every inch of her, and she had been thrilled at his reaction.

Which, of course, was also superficial.

'What do you mean, *playing with fire*?' she asked demurely.

'You know exactly what I mean.'

A sense of heady power surged through her. Whatever ups and downs she had survived in her life, she had always lived within a comfort zone of her own making. She had formed an image in her head of the sort of guy she would eventually meet and had carved out a future based on that image: a nice guy, supportive, safe…the opposite of her appalling stepfather. She had known what she'd wanted to do with her life and had applied all her determination to succeed in her field to the exclusion of anything that might remotely have resembled taking a big risk. So yes, for the first time in her life, she was playing with fire.

Giddy with excitement, Sammy gazed up at Rafael and parted her lips. Her nostrils flared, breathing in whatever woody scent he was wearing, something earthy that went straight to her head.

'You want me to kiss you?' Rafael ground out. 'Because, if I do, it won't be because I'm playing to an audience.'

He kissed her. The world disappeared. She felt her whole body slacken as she melted into the kiss, into his arms, her hands weaving into his hair, completely lost in the moment. She was dazed when he pulled back and, when their eyes met, she knew that he wasn't in control either.

But people were watching, and she adjusted her skirt sheepishly as they both turned to face all the eyes that were glued to their moment of passion.

'Now, that's a couple who mean business,' Robert Kendrick said with a smile as he raised his glass.

Rafael had his arm around her shoulders but this time it was different. She could feel the tension of his hold and she knew he didn't want to let her go.

'Not like me,' Rafael said gruffly.

'That's what love can do to a guy,' Kendrick said, still grinning broadly.

'Almost makes a guy forget,' Rafael returned, 'that there's a certain booking at a club for us! We'd better get going.'

The kiss stayed with Sammy. It was like a bee sting on her lips as the evening progressed. All the common sense she had invoked to prevent this rush of desire had been thrown through the window.

This evening, she was all about Rafael. The music was sensual and loud, and she let herself go to it, swaying and seducing on the dance floor and loving the way he couldn't take his eyes off her.

She forgot all about Victoria, barely glancing in her

direction, but, with female instinct, she still knew that the other woman would not like what she saw. For the first time, someone else was competing for attention. She wasn't the only young, strutting beauty in between the staid, impeccably dressed older women. Sammy discovered that she relished the sensation.

'Let's get you home,' Rafael whispered into her ear as the evening drew to a close. The music had slowed and he was pressed against her, his hard body moving rhythmically to the music, his thigh pushing between hers and his hand on her waist, guiding her to his beat.

'I can't wait.'

'Are you saying what I think you're saying?'

'Depends what you think I'm saying.'

'Sammy…'

'I know. You don't have to spell it out, Rafael. This isn't about two people who plan on having a relationship. This is about the here and now, and I don't understand it any better than you probably do.'

She moaned softly as his hand dipped lower, nestling just above her buttocks. Through the flimsy fabric of her shirt, she could feel its heat burning into her.

'You're not wearing a bra,' he murmured. 'I like that.'

'Do you, now?'

'My imagination has been freewheeling ever since we got here.'

'So has mine.' Sammy couldn't believe she'd actually said that. She felt a rush of daring recklessness.

'I want to get you into bed.'

The music stopped, and they reluctantly pulled apart,

but remained close enough for him to say shakily to her, 'But I'll ask that question again when the bed is within sight, because when the music is blaring and drinks have been had words can sometimes be rashly spoken.'

'Maybe I'll be saying the same thing to you,' Sammy murmured, casting a lingering look at his darkly handsome face.

Piled into a car with another of the couples on the way back, Sammy sat in a state of simmering excitement. In her head, she replayed the evening, from standing in front of that mirror and looking at herself in clothes she usually would never have dreamt of wearing in a million years. Tonight had been the culmination of what she had felt the second she had walked into Rafael's office, all guns blazing, to confront him about the hotel.

She had felt the breath catch in her throat then when she'd seen him and, even though she'd tried her best to stifle that wild, crazy physical response to him, she hadn't been able to. It had grown under tropical skies and this game they were playing had nurtured it into a full-blown, irresistible craving.

He was forbidden, for all sorts of reasons, and she knew that. He was a guy whose goals in life were so different from hers, a complex guy who didn't want to settle down and who scorned the straightforward path she had always envisaged for herself. Yet this was the first time she had discovered how alluring the forbidden fruit could be.

She rested her head against his shoulder in the back

of the car and gazed out at the scenery flashing past. The windows were rolled down and the breeze blowing through the car was warm. The foliage at the side of the road was dense with huge, flowering bushes and tall, thin coconut trees. Rising up the side of the hills were bright squares of light where wooden houses nestled into the forest.

Looking up, Sammy could make out the pinpricks of stars against the velvety black sky. There was no light pollution at all here.

She sighed and vaguely thought about what waited for her back in England. Her career would begin to take off. Looking for somewhere to buy would be hectic yet enjoyable, because there would be no concerns about money. She should have been thinking about that, and making plans, but it all felt very far away. The only thing in her head right now was the man against whom she was resting.

The cars all arrived at the villa at the same time and there were sleepy goodnights from everyone. Victoria was there, sulky and lurking slightly behind Clement. Sammy ignored her, and she noticed Rafael did as well, confining his brief conversation to Clement while his ex glared and fulminated. Somewhere during the course of the evening, Victoria had seemed to stop trying to dazzle. Now she looked a little sad in her drooping silver sequinned dress that barely skirted her thighs and the high heels that made her tower over everyone in the party.

Sammy and Rafael headed up to their suite and Sammy felt the thud of anticipation like a drumbeat inside her. He was holding her hand and, as he pushed open the door, he turned to her.

'Okay—question time.'

'I'll go first.' She leaned against the wall and gazed up at him with a sexy half-smile. 'Sure you're going to be all right with this?'

'Let me think about that,' Rafael murmured, flattening his hands on either side of her so that she was deliciously caged in.

'I mean,' Sammy elaborated huskily, 'I wouldn't want you to get all upset because you think I've taken advantage of you after all that dancing and drinking...' She walked her fingers over his chest and then stroked the side of his face. Her heart skipped a beat as his eyes darkened with desire.

He held her hand and grazed his mouth against her knuckles.

'I'll do my best to keep regrets to the minimum...'

'Good, and so will I. Because we're here, Rafael, and I don't think I've ever wanted anyone in my life as much as I want you right now. I don't understand it, and believe me I know it's not going anywhere—which is a very good thing—but I can't seem to help myself.'

'Ditto.'

And then he kissed her, one hand still propped against the wall, the other teasing the underside of her breast through the stretchy material of the vest.

Sammy groaned. The wetness between her legs was driving her crazy. She wanted to guide his hand there, wanted to pull aside her panties so that he could touch her and drive her even more crazy. He lifted her as though she weighed nothing and she wrapped her legs around him as they managed to make it to the bedroom.

'I think your place rather than mine,' he teased, nuzzling her ear. 'Somehow, a bed is a lot more appealing than a sofa.'

'I don't care where we go.' Sammy groaned truthfully. 'Just as long as we get there quickly.'

'You won't be getting anywhere quickly,' he murmured huskily in return. 'At least, not if I have my wicked way.'

He was true to his word. He took his time, leaving the lights off so that the only light came from the moon casting shadows and angles though the shutters into the bedroom. The fan overhead was a pleasing background whirr, picking up from where the night sounds outside left off.

He deposited her gently on the bed and she immediately wriggled up against the pillows so that she could look at him in open appreciation as he got undressed. He was magnificent. Her mouth fell open as he stripped off his tee-shirt, revealing a tightly muscled torso and powerful arms, his chest darkened with hair. Her breathing was uneven as he continued the striptease without an ounce of embarrassment. His boxers were black and she could see the very visible outline of his erection. She held her breath as the boxers came down and he casually touched himself, stroking himself as he lazily strolled towards her.

'Enjoying the view?' he ground out, settling on the

mattress but, rather than lying next to her, he knelt over her.

'V-very much so,' Sammy managed to stutter, eyes glued to the mesmerising sight of him stroking himself. 'If only I had a camera.'

'What a wicked thought...'

Rafael smiled. This level of intensity and excitement felt like something he'd been waiting for all his life, freed from all the restrictions he was so accustomed to laying down in his relationships. She was the one laying down the rules, and the rules were *his* rules. How much more perfect could a situation get?

Gazing at him with green, slumberous eyes, she was the epitome of everything desirable and, with a groan of abandon, he pushed up the flimsy wraparound skirt. She had satin-soft thighs and a flat stomach. He gently eased off her underwear, but he didn't have the patience to take off the rest of her clothes. Instead, he bent to bury his head between her thighs, and the first taste of her was as sweet as nectar. He flicked his tongue along her wet slit and found the bud of her clitoris. He teased it until she was panting and writhing against his mouth.

Taking it slowly, something he excelled at, was beyond his reach. He'd never wanted anyone as badly as he wanted her and the fact that she felt the same way about him was even more of a turn-on. He couldn't get her clothes off fast enough and neither could she. Together they flung her stuff over the side of the bed, and he had one moment of excruciating pleasure as he reared up to look at her naked body.

She was so slight, so smooth. Her breasts were small and perfectly shaped, barely a handful, and he could practically span her waist with his hands; yet there was a well-toned strength to her ballerina-like body that spoke of the physically testing career she had made her own, always on her feet and seldom slowing down.

Everything about her struck him as perfect. He tasted her everywhere. He licked her breasts and suckled on her ripe, pink nipples until she was begging him to take her. He stroked her belly and kissed her so that she was senseless with desire. Every second of touching was agony because all he wanted to do was be inside her.

When he could stand it no longer, he reached for protection. His fingers were so shaky that he could barely rip open the foil packet. Sinking into her was bliss. He'd died and gone to heaven. She was tight around him, and her body moved in sync with his so that, as he arched back to orgasm, she too tightened and stiffened, moving in unison with him.

Rafael came on a shudder that forced out a groan of satisfaction and then, sated, he rolled off her and lay beside her.

'No regrets?' he murmured, stroking her hair from her damp forehead, and she drowsily smiled back at him.

'None at all. I never thought I could do this…never thought I could sleep with a guy I don't plan on having any kind of relationship with. But… I just did…and I've never felt so liberated. So, regrets? None…'

CHAPTER EIGHT

RAFAEL LOOKED AT Sammy from under his lashes as she unpacked the picnic he had had prepared for them. He was playing truant from real life and enjoying it. His guests had left the day before. Everything had been signed, sealed and delivered and he had breathed a sigh of relief. Victoria might have fumed and simmered in the background, but she had heeded his thinly veiled words of warning, and had decided to take on board where her bread was buttered.

Rock the boat, he had implied, *and say goodbye to the lifestyle you've got with Clement.*

He hadn't worked out what he was going to do about Sammy but, the minute she had become his lover, the rules of the game had drastically changed. There was no longer pretend-touching for the sake of their captive audience—it was real touching, and the real touching was mind blowing.

He hadn't worked out why she felt so addictive but he guessed that it was because there was no pressure on him to do anything but live in the moment. She made no demands. She never mentioned anything about a future, and never uttered those terminal words: *where do we go from here...?*

She hadn't dropped a single hint that she wanted to carry on seeing him once they returned to England. Had she wondered? He had no idea. She was so unashamedly open with him about everything, so unimpressed by his wealth and his status, so sexually curious and enthusiastic...and yet something about her remained carefully concealed.

He would have suggested continuing what they had, but in fact remaining on the island after everyone left had been suggested by Clement, thereby putting him in the fortunate position of just having to go along with it.

'You've worked to produce great food,' Clement had said the evening before over their last supper. 'Now you two need to take a little time to yourselves without having to think about us all. You should stay on here for a few days. I'm sure—' he had winked at Rafael '—the world can spare you for a week or so.'

Rafael had laughed and slapped Clement on the back. Sammy, though, had remained silent for a few seconds, seeming to mull over the suggestion. He'd had to damp down his initial irritation at her response, and had had to laugh at his ego, which was telling him that any other woman would have bitten his hand off to stay on for another week.

Since when had his own invincibility gone to his head? he had asked himself. Since when had he had the expectation that any woman would want to put herself out for him? Was he really that arrogant?

So he'd impatiently laughed at himself, even though he'd been stupidly piqued by her deliberation. Then, when she'd smiled, nodded and glanced at him sideways with that sexy little look of hers, he'd wanted to punch the air with satisfaction.

'Do my humble picnic offerings meet your high standards?' he asked now, his dark gaze lingering on her face. He was stretched out on the oversized towel they had brought, hands folded behind his head.

He couldn't have picked a better spot. The cove was a fifteen-minute boat ride away and was completely private. Now that it was just the two of them and his time wasn't committed to other people, he wanted to show her the best the island could offer, and it didn't come better than this.

Coconut trees sat against a backdrop of lush, tropical mountains. It was just a tiny inlet but the turquoise water was very calm, like a pool, and the sand was like caster sugar. The boat he had driven was anchored to the left and bobbing gently on the water.

She had oohed and aahed when they'd arrived, and he'd felt a real kick of pleasure, a desire to take her to more places just so that he could see that smile on her face as she looked around.

She was rummaging in the picnic basket and wearing a very similar expression of wonderment. Rafael smiled and propped himself up on one elbow to watch her.

'It's perfect. I like the champagne. Can you be done for being drunk and disorderly behind the wheel of a boat?'

She glanced at him and Rafael felt that familiar tug

in his groin as his libido kicked into gear. *Those eyes… that perfect mouth…* Just thinking about how she could turn him on made him horny. He thought about her kisses and how she could lick him in ways that made him lose control within seconds.

'Thankfully, there's no traffic in this particular part of the Atlantic. Stop fussing there and come and sit by me. You're beginning to go pink. I want to rub some sun cream on you—make sure you don't get burnt.'

'That's very considerate of you.'

'I'm an extremely considerate person.'

'It's so beautiful here, Rafael. I don't know how you can resist coming as often as you can.'

'Time is money.'

'And doing nothing is good for the soul. Especially if you're doing nothing in a place like this.'

'Are you beginning to think that you might want to stay on and do the six months here after all?' he teased, eyes darkening as she sashayed towards him.

He intended to have that prissy black one-piece off her before too long, but right now it was pleasant playing with images of what was underneath it: those pale, small breasts; those perfect rosy nipples that he couldn't get enough of; her flat, smooth stomach.

'Maybe!' She laughed back at him.

Rafael watched as she settled on the towel next to him and shoved on her sunglasses so that, when their eyes met, he couldn't see what she was thinking.

'Maybe? You're not being serious, are you?'

'Why not? Before I came here, I had no idea what it

was going to be like, but everyone is so friendly, and honestly…? Who in their right mind could resist the temptation to spend a little time out here? It's not as though I'd get the chance to come back here any time soon.'

Sammy lay down on the towel and closed her eyes but she knew that Rafael had sat up and was staring down at her.

When Clement had said that they should take a few days' break on the island to enjoy themselves, having spent the week catering to the needs of clients in their various ways, she had waited to take the lead from Rafael. She'd wondered how he would react to that suggestion. He hadn't said a word about what would happen next with them and their situation. They'd been ensconced in a bubble, in which the sizzling excitement of touching one another for show had exploded into the real thing, and she'd been carried away to cloud nine.

But she wasn't an idiot. He was only in it for a bit of passing fun. He wasn't going to take things any further, and over her dead body was she going to give any hint that the thought of walking away from this fantastic experience made her feel sick. It wasn't as though she'd invested feelings in him, was it? She'd known the rules of the game from day one and she wasn't stupid.

If she wanted more of him than a few days out here, then it was just because he'd opened a door in her and she was enjoying the experience. She'd committed to having fun with her eyes wide open, and she wasn't going to suddenly turn into a martyr and start feeling angst about her decision. He might not fit the bill of her 'for ever' guy, but he was making her see that there was no crime when it came to having a bit of fun.

So she'd made a show of thinking carefully when that suggestion had been made before slowly nodding and agreeing, yes, why not stay on a while longer? She wasn't playing hard to get because there was nothing to get. She was looking after herself because she knew what he was like, and she wasn't going to end up as another of his casualties.

'You have things to do in England.'

'I know.' She opened her eyes and peered at him from behind the safety of her sunglasses. 'But you've shown me that taking a walk on the wild side can be a good thing.'

'How so?'

'Well…' Sammy sat up so that they were at eye level with each other, and she tilted the sunglasses on her forehead to meet his gaze squarely. 'When I first saw you again, you were the sort of guy I instantly disliked.'

'Thank you straight away for the compliment.'

'You can't blame me. You'd swiped the rug from under my feet.'

'Not to mention having spent some of my youth making sure your brother hopped on the bandwagon.'

'Actually,' Sammy mused, briefly shading her eyes and staring off at the ocean, 'I thought about what you said and I think you're right. You didn't so much lead Colin astray as allowed his rebellion to find a voice, which was probably a good thing for him in the end.' She sighed. 'He may have skipped a year, but it was the best thing that could have happened, because he returned in a better place.'

'That's a generous admission from you,' Rafael said truthfully.

'You're a considerate person offering to rub sunblock on my back, and I'm a generous person admitting that you were right about Colin. What saints the pair of us are.'

Rafael grinned, then looked at her in a slightly different way, his eyes lazy and appreciative.

His hands were nowhere near her but her whole body shivered, as though he'd physically touched her. Her nipples tightened and there was a wave of intense sensation that washed through her, making her mouth dry and her pupils dilate. She felt hot and sluggish.

The pull of lust was something she had massively underestimated—that was something she was very quickly realising. Right now, she just wanted to dump the serious conversation, lean into him, feel the coolness of his mouth against hers and put his hands where she wanted them to be. But she could feel the urge to say something that would paper over that cracks of apprehension that he was beginning to *matter*. Not just as a guy she was having fun with, but as a guy who was complex and three-dimensional, demanding more than just a romp in the sack.

'You were telling me how much you disliked me at first sight.' Rafael returned her to the present and to what she wanted to get across to him—that she was as casual about what was happening between them as he was. 'Or maybe I should say *second* sight, because you weren't exactly a member of my fan club back in the day.'

'The waiting list was long for that particular role,' Sammy said drily. 'From what I remember.'

'And would you have joined the waiting list if it hadn't been as long?'

'No.'

He burst out laughing. 'I like the way you tell it like it is without any consideration for a man's fragile ego.'

'You have the ego of a steel vault.'

'But moving on from the compliments...'

'I learnt a lot from what my mother went through,' Sammy told him thoughtfully. 'She had such a rough ride of it after Dad died and after she married that awful man. She married in haste and repented at leisure. It gave me time to work out that love was something you should never rush into. That you might think a guy is going to be good for you but, unless you really know what you're looking for, you can so easily end up making a big mistake.'

'You're going round the houses here, Sammy.'

He reached forward to stroke a lazy finger over her mouth and then along her shoulders, taking his time. 'You have amazing shoulders.'

'Stop distracting me, Rafael.'

'Why? I like distracting you. In fact, I think I could make a career choice out of doing that.'

'I'm trying to explain...'

'Tell me.'

His voice was husky and seductive and didn't give the

impression that he was hanging onto her every word. It gave the impression that the only thing he wanted to do was tug off her swimsuit and make love to her.

Sammy shuddered because she wanted that badly herself. It was unsettling to realise how much of a hold her body had over her brain and how vulnerable that made her feel. She frowned, trying to connect disparate threads of thought, but her head seemed to be all over the place.

He just had to touch her or even look at her with those dark, sexy eyes and all of a sudden she couldn't think straight. That was a dangerous place to be and the feel of that danger was like a feathery touch against her skin.

'I've been very careful when it comes to guys.' She cleared her throat and propped her sunglasses back on because it felt safer. 'I mean, I've gone through life not wanting to make any mistakes.'

'But you had boyfriends…yet you're not married. So doesn't that imply that mistakes were made along the way?' Thankfully he stopped the tactile exploration and looked at her with his head tilted to one side and his expression serious.

'One serious boyfriend,' Sammy admitted. 'I thought it was going somewhere. We both did, but in the end it fizzled out. There were no hard feelings and we're still friends on social media. I'll always have a soft spot for him in my heart but he wasn't the one for me.'

'It all sounds very flat.'

'What do you mean?'

'Two earnest people trying to make something work… holding hands, gazing into each other's eyes and waiting for the spark and then nothing…but good friends still, like brother and sister.'

'It was nothing like that!' Sammy protested vehemently, thinking that that was exactly what it had been like.

'Sure about that?' He raised his eyebrows and grinned. 'I'm guessing this is where I come in?'

'As a matter of fact, it is. You showed me that I could have a fling without it meaning anything at all and enjoy myself.' He was still grinning, which got on her nerves, but at least he'd stopped touching her so that she could get her thoughts in order. 'You didn't tick any of the boxes—you still don't.'

'The boxes being…? No, let me guess—is reliable one of them? Diligent, hard-working? If you say "considerate", then you'd have to admit that I happen to tick at least one of those boxes…'

Sammy ignored that interjection. Those boxes were indeed the very ones she had but, said aloud, they seemed dull and boring.

'You don't tick any of the boxes,' she returned, ignoring the grin as she'd ignored the interjection. 'You're pure fun that's not going anywhere, and you've done me a favour by making me see that a situation without a future doesn't necessarily mean that it's a situation I shouldn't have.'

'Glad to be of service.'

'It's good to be getting that out of my system.'

'Having fun?'

'Being reckless.'

'Am I as reckless as it gets for you?'

'You are, as a matter of fact.'

'Good. I like that and, now that you've got that out of your system, shall we get down and dirty with the recklessness?'

'It's so hot. We could go swim, I suppose—not that I'm much of a swimmer.'

'I swim like a fish. You just have to hang on to me. We need to get in the right mood for swimming, though. Maybe a little bit of that recklessness you were describing a minute ago? If I'm to be your teacher in all things rash and daring, then I think it's only fair that I do a thorough job of it before you return to the safety of your comfort zone and Mr Dull waiting on the horizon.'

He tugged down the sensible strap of her swimsuit, traced where the strap had been, and the little indentation it had made in her shoulder, and then let his fingers drift down to circle the jut of her nipple against the stretchy material.

Sammy surrendered.

She opened herself up to him, arm flung over her face as he took his time disposing of the swimsuit. She had to do her fair share of wriggling out of it to help things along, but she did, because need was getting the better of her.

The way he touched her made her feel as though she were being touched for the first time, as though his clever fingers and his questing mouth had managed to access parts of her she'd never known existed. He nuzzled the softness between her small breasts before settling on an engorged nipple and tugging at it so that sighs turned to little cries and whimpers.

'You're beautiful; you really are,' he murmured huskily.

'You're just saying that.'

'I never say stuff I don't mean. I can't tell you how much you turn me on. Just thinking of you gives me an erection.'

Sammy sighed happily and let him explore her. He touched her everywhere. In the space of a few days, he seemed to have familiarised himself with every inch of her body. Yes, she knew what to expect, and yet every flick of his tongue on her skin was a revelation.

He held her hips as he contoured her belly button with delicate licks. Sammy groaned and pushed her fingers through his thick, dark hair. She was barely aware of him reaching for protection. He never failed to use it. She could have told him that she was on the pill and he would still have protected himself. He was very, very careful about making sure that no one could pin him down for any reason whatsoever.

She welcomed him in. Her whole body sank into the utter pleasure of feeling his bigness fill her up, and when he came it was with a convulsive shudder. He took her with him, took her to the same soaring heights and left her weak as a kitten afterwards.

When he rolled off her, he lay there for a few seconds and linked his fingers with hers in a gesture that was very intimate and casual at the same time. Sammy stared up at the sky, in tune with him and loving the way he was absently holding her hand.

Thinking that…thinking what?…that this was really paradise? And not just because of the blue sea, the white sand and the swaying coconut trees. She could get picture-postcard stuff all over the world. What made *this* picture-postcard special was the man lying next to her, seeing the same sky as she but probably thinking very different thoughts.

She looked sideways and her heart constricted. The mantra she had been repeating to herself suddenly felt hollow and different thoughts began creeping in—a different view of what had been happening inside her over the past few days. She thought of the way this man made her laugh. Even before they'd become lovers, when they'd been playing the game in front of his clients, her skin had tingled where he had touched it and her heart had raced when he'd glanced at her.

She didn't believe in this kind of love, she frantically told herself. She had her checklist—the very checklist she'd only just finished telling him all about! Except… had she done that for his benefit or for her own?

She stood up suddenly and began putting on the swimsuit.

'Where are you going?'

'For a swim.'

'I thought you weren't a strong swimmer?'

'I'm going to paddle. I won't get into any trouble if I paddle.'

'Wait, Sammy.'

Rafael leapt up behind her and stuck on his trunks as she made her way to the edge of the sea. He circled her arm, tugging her back.

'What's wrong?'

'Sorry?' Sammy shielded her eyes and looked up at him. The water swirling round her ankles was warm and clear. Her pulse was racing, and her head had suddenly started spinning stories about involvement with the last guy on the planet she should be involved with. She resisted reaching out to touch his face.

'Have I said something to…upset you?' Rafael raked his fingers through his hair and shifted awkwardly, his other hand still circling her arm.

He looked touchingly concerned but Sammy knew better than to feed into something that wasn't there.

'No. Just…phew…it's baking hot.'

She flapped her hand in a fan-like motion and smiled. Should she start making noises about returning to England? He'd mentioned staying on for a few days, and she'd been happy to go along with that vague timeline, but should she now put a number on those days and take control of the situation instead of drifting?

'You swim out, Rafael. I'll sit on the edge here. It's nice. I can watch you swim and show off how fit you are.'

He relaxed and grinned. 'Well now, I admit I can rise to that challenge.'

'I'm warning you, though, that if you start floundering out there you're on your own.' He was so beautiful, so smart…so damned irresistible. Was this just fun or was it something else?

'Understood, but that's never going to happen. I'm not a guy who flounders.'

'But you *are* a guy who brags.'

He was still grinning, all trace of concern at her change of mood gone. 'If you must know, and to brag a little bit more, I forced myself to learn how to swim as soon as we moved to Yorkshire. I decided that there were no hurdles I wasn't capable of overcoming, so I went to the pool a few times, listened in on a swimming coach giving lessons to a couple of old ladies and then went to that lake in the woods—you know the one? I jumped in and hoped that I'd remember the instructions from that coach.'

'You're kidding.'

'It was a lot more educational than school. Besides, what was the worst that could happen?'

'Death by drowning?'

'Yet here I am.' He burst out laughing and dipped to kiss her on the mouth until her head was reeling. 'But just in case I do flounder,' he murmured, 'you'd better make sure you don't take your eyes off me.'

Sammy retreated back to the beach, sat on the towel and watched him. He struck out, lean body cutting through the blue, blue water with powerful, even strokes. Surely he hadn't learned to swim like that from eaves-dropping on a swimming coach at the age of fifteen and then jumping in a lake? But then, he was the guy who would never allow himself to fail. He would never *flounder*.

And that included floundering in his private life. She knew his back story, and knew how it had impacted on him and how it channelled all his decisions about relationships. There was no weakness inside him when it came to women. He wouldn't have any thoughts about this situation between them that had started as a charade and was now…whatever it was. A pleasant distraction for him…and for her, something that was beginning to feel a lot more than that.

She didn't want to keep thinking about that.

Instead, she got her phone and was playing on it when it buzzed. Sammy was so surprised that she almost didn't pick up, but her mother's name flashed on the screen. Why was her mother calling her? She and her mother messaged daily, but phone calls were usually reserved for birthdays and *situations*. Situations that often involved her brother and whatever news her mother felt she had to convey *urgently*—usually, Colin would later tell Sammy nothing had been truly urgent at all—or else to pass on some gossip about a neighbour that likewise 'couldn't wait'.

So she picked up the call with some hesitation. She sat up and gazed blankly out to the horizon, into which Rafael seemed to have vanished in record time. He was now making back for land, swimming back as rhythmically as he had swum out. Her mind was drifting but the minute she heard her mother's voice she sat up straighter.

'Sammy, darling, I'm so glad I got hold of you.'

She sat up straighter still, then stood up, because she knew from the tone of her mother's voice that whatever conversation was about to take place wasn't going to be a good one.

* * *

Rafael was heading back, having resisted the temptation to disappear into the great blue yonder. He hadn't been exaggerating when he'd told Sammy that he'd learnt to swim by literally throwing himself in at the deep end. It had all been part of his anger at life all those years ago. He'd loved to push the boundaries, never more so than when it came to swimming; he'd bunked off school too many times to count so that he could go down to that lake and freeze his butt off swimming as though his life depended on it.

He'd never stopped enjoying the freedom it afforded him. He had a magnificent indoor swimming pool in the basement of his mansion in London and swimming in it was the best therapy anyone could have. So it had been tempting to push the boat out today, but he knew that Sammy would end up getting worried about him if she lost sight of him.

He didn't know *how* he knew that. He just did, and it gave him a warm feeling inside that was pleasurable, if a little confusing. He'd dated women in the past, and spent months with the same woman, and yet had never felt this weird thing he felt with Sammy.

He *knew* her. At least, it felt like that to him. It was unsettling but he liked it, even though there was just the merest hint of alarm bells ringing in the distance somewhere.

Now, as he glimpsed her in between strokes, he got the feeling that something was up. For starters, she was on the phone. Who was calling her? He knew that she'd told her mother something vague about staying out on the island for a bit longer, but that everything had been sorted with the work placement. He'd been in the bedroom when she'd made the call. She'd strolled through the room, completely naked, idly pausing to look at something or other and talking in a low, soft, reassuring voice while he'd lain on the bed watching her and making suggestive expressions while she tried not to laugh.

He reached shore just as she was ending the call and the minute he saw her face he knew something was off.

'Talk to me,' he said urgently, reaching for a towel and, after a quick dry, slinging it over his shoulders as he walked towards her.

'I was just on the phone to my mother, Rafael.'

'And you look as though you need something fortifying. Go sit under that tree in the shade. I'll bring you some champagne. You're white as a sheet.'

He felt a sickening jolt of panic as he busied himself with the champagne, which was ice-cold in its frozen sleeve. Whatever was going on, he was going to make sure she knew that she could count on him.

Hell, what if there had been a death in the family? He felt nauseous just thinking about it but, as he approached her with the two glasses and the champagne bottle, his expression was inscrutable.

She was sitting on one of the over-sized towels they had brought with them and had drawn her knees up to her chest. Her short hair was ruffled by the breeze and still dry because she hadn't actually dived into the water at all. He'd noticed that from the distance, looking back at her when he'd paused for breath, and had absently thought that it might be fun to teach her how to swim. Everyone should know how to swim, and he did have his own private pool, after all.

'Okay, Sammy. Drink this and then tell me what's going on with your mother. Is she okay? Colin…is he okay? Has something happened to either of them?'

Sammy leaned towards him, as if sensing his strength and wanting to be supported by it.

'She's found out.'

'Found out what?'

'About us. Victoria got in touch with her. She phoned really upset because she was told that we're engaged and that you're not the kind of guy I should be getting engaged to.'

'How the hell did Victoria find your mother?'

'I guess it was just a case of following the clues. In the spiel on my website, I reference my mum quite a bit— that she's my inspiration. I suppose she got hold of my mum's name and then just did a little detective work.'

'So she got to screw me over after all,' he said grimly. 'She might not have gone public but going private was just as destructive.'

'She gave Mum a rundown of your history and the fact that you've never committed to anyone, and of course my mother is super-protective when it comes to me. She kind of made it her mission to instil common sense in me when it came to guys. So for her to find out that I'm apparently engaged after five seconds, and to a man who plays the field and is proud of it… She's devastated.'

'Jesus, Sammy.' He held her gaze. 'What did you tell her?'

Rafael stiffened, every damning word driving a knife deep into a part of him he hadn't known existed. A part of him that wasn't as invincible as he had always cared to think. He was that man: the man who had never committed; the man who played the field and had always done so without a conscience. The guy who had figured that to be upfront from the start was to deliver immunity from the consequences of broken relationships. To hear those words delivered casually by the woman now speaking them was to be judged and found wanting in a way that cut to the core.

'I told her that I could take care of myself and that she wasn't to worry.' Sammy drank what was left of the champagne in one long swallow that made her splutter. 'And when it ends,' she continued in a rush, 'I can tell her that it was a learning curve and that I'll never rush into anything ever again, but that I have no regrets.'

'No fizzling out? I thought you were a fan of the gradual tapering off when a relationship starts going pear-shaped,' Rafael said.

'No—no fizzling anything. I'll tell her that I discovered, once we left this paradise, that you were someone I couldn't live with in the real world. I'll tell her that you were my adventure.'

Rafael gazed at her long and hard. What was really going through her head? What was going through his was terrifying because he knew that more than his body was involved in this dangerous game. His heart had become involved as well. But did she feel the same? It was impossible to tell.

'We should give her time to digest everything.' He lowered his eyes.

'What are you saying?'

'We stay here for a little longer. I can oversee the hotel and work remotely. We can let the dust settle so that when we return to England your mother is less…devastated and more philosophical about what you…*we*… might have to tell her. I won't let you break that kind of news on your own.'

'We stay here?'

'And you …' he smiled crookedly but his dark eyes remained serious '…you might find that I really am the kind of guy you could never live with in the real world…'

CHAPTER NINE

SAMMY WANTED TO return to Yorkshire immediately. She could easily imagine her mother worried and fretful and wondering what the hell was going on.

There was no way she could ever think that a sudden engagement was ever going to be anything but trouble. Even if there'd been no engagement—if Sammy had said in passing that she and Rafael were going out, maybe casually dating, or had been out for a cup of coffee together—her mother would still have had her antennae quivering with suspicion. Rich guy and speedy attraction…add those two things together and what she'd get was *trouble*.

Her mother's past had taught her enough about chancers for her to be instinctively wary of someone like Rafael. Frankly, to be wary of any guy showing up and suddenly becoming an item in her daughter's life after five minutes. Victoria's call would have set the wheels in motion, and mention of an engagement would have been the icing on a very bad-tasting cake.

Rafael, though, calmly talked her out of it as they sat on that beach towel, each staring out at the blue ocean whilst working their way to a solution to the sudden complication that had arisen.

'We can easily stay here for another couple of weeks, by which time your mother will have calmed down,' he said.

'You don't know my mother.'

'No one can stay anxious for weeks on end. After a while, it dulls.'

'Again, you don't know my mother. After our stepfather disappeared from the scene, Mum suddenly took on a ton of guilt for the massive wrong decision she had made in marrying him in the first place. She made it her mission to make sure that I, in particular, didn't do anything rash when it came to my emotions.'

'What about Colin?'

'She automatically assumed that Colin would be able to look after himself.' Sammy half-smiled. 'Don't ask. At any rate, she drummed it into me that I should always be careful never to be taken advantage of.'

'Is that why you developed that checklist for boring men?'

'"Kind, thoughtful and reliable" doesn't automatically mean boring.'

'If you say so.'

'Anyway, I could stay away for a week or a month or a year and my mother would still be worried sick that I was making a mistake. I think we should go back to England and tell her immediately that the whole engagement thing was a fabrication.'

'We could do that.'

But then he turned to look at her, reached and touched her, just a light, feathery touch that had made her melt.

'But Sammy, let's be honest with one another. The engagement might have been a fabrication but what we have together—this thing between us—that's real.' He paused, frowned and took a sudden step back. 'The passion, I mean. The flame that can't be put out. Don't tell me that *that's* not real.'

'Yes, well…'

'Sure, we could go back over there, and we could go into a lengthy explanation about Victoria and Clement and pretending to be the couple we weren't at the time. Shall I tell you what your mother would think of that?'

'Can I stop you?'

'Any time you like.'

'Tell me. What would Mum think if we showed up and told her the truth, now that you seem to have a crystal ball?'

'She'd think that after everything she's told you, after every word of warning she's issued over the years, you've let yourself be seduced into a lie by a guy who messes women around.'

'I've told her that you're not the man Victoria described.' Sammy broke eye contact, but he'd made a point, and it was one she hadn't considered. Of course her mother would be disappointed, and would think that she had rushed headlong into lust with the wrong guy. She'd remember Rafael the youthful rebel, the boy who had led Colin astray, and all her defences would shoot into position.

Sammy had truthfully told her mother that Rafael wasn't the guy Victoria had made him out to be; that he wasn't the guy the tabloid papers portrayed who moved from woman to woman, picking up and putting down like a spoilt kid in a toy shop.

She uneasily ran through the sincerity in her voice as she'd waxed lyrical about Rafael to her mother, persuading her out of her anxiety and persuading herself into the dawning realisation of something she must have known for a while. The realisation that she had fallen for a guy who hadn't returned the favour—not when it came to love, which was so very different from passion—and that she'd gone and done the very thing she'd always told herself she would never do.

A sick feeling swirled inside her.

Forget about her mother and her disappointment if they rushed back to England so that they could spill the beans on the little game they had set in motion—one look at her and Caroline Payne would know that her daughter had fallen for Rafael. So much for all her teachings.

'What did you tell her?' Rafael asked her curiously.

'That Victoria was a woman with an axe to grind and that she would do anything to make sure you paid the price for dumping her—woman scorned and all that stuff.'

'Hmm.'

'But I see what you mean.'

'That it's better for us to stay here for a bit until things flatten out?'

'It would be an opportunity for me to slowly begin to

tell Mum that perhaps I got carried away by being out here...that lust got the better of me, but that everything she'd ever said about using my head when choosing a guy was right, because bit by bit I could see that you weren't the one for me.'

'Not dull enough,' Rafael murmured in agreement.

'In the end, common sense would win through and by the time I return to Yorkshire Mum would be fine with it all.'

'And you haven't thought of the other upside to us remaining out here.'

'Which is what?'

In her head, she had been dealing with the roller-coaster ride of emotions that had swamped her without even really realising: *she was in love with Rafael.*

She loved everything about him, from the way he laughed to the way he touched her, to the things he said that made her think and the way he teased her until she was laughing at herself with him.

'That we exhaust this,' he said.

'This?'

'This crazy passion we have for one another. It'll subside. Crazy passion always comes with a sell-by date. But, if we were to walk away from it before it naturally goes, then both of us would always be left with a want that hadn't had a chance to be satisfied, an itch still waiting to be scratched. We stay here two weeks, perhaps even a bit longer, and we see this through to the end. No dissatisfaction left because that itch hasn't been scratched.'

Sammy nodded, lost in her own thoughts and sadly thinking that, whereas her feelings for him ran too deep to quantify, his feelings for her were best summed up as an itch to be scratched.

But she needed time, and a couple more weeks here would give her the time she needed.

Rafael strolled through the glass sliding doors of the villa that gave out to the landscaped gardens at the back. To the right the swimming pool was lit up with lights that were cleverly strung between swaying palm trees and threaded through some of the dense foliage. The blue of the pool was very dark, a dappled swirl of shadows casting stripes across the flat, still surface.

The veranda here was very wide and circled the entirety of the back, wide enough for clusters of chairs, tables and potted plants. Beyond the lit section the landscape disappeared into tropical darkness, which was dense, and pierced here and there with fireflies and the gentle swoop of bats diving in search of food.

Sammy was in the kitchen. Standing out here with a glass of wine in his hand, he smiled to himself at the thought of her shooing him away, telling him that she wanted to surprise him with a special dinner. He liked the way she'd been pink from the heat of the kitchen, her whole body radiating satisfaction at doing something she enjoyed.

The plan to remain on the island had been a good one. They'd been here for ten days in total, and he knew from the conversations they'd had that her mother had come down from the sharp anxiety she had felt when she'd first found out about their so-called engagement.

For a brief second, he frowned because something else occurred to him: where was the boredom? When was that due to set in—shouldn't it be round about now?

Sure, he had had longer-lasting women in his life in the past but, thinking about it, he'd never spent so much undiluted time with any of them. He and Sammy were practically together on a twenty-four-seven basis. They'd fallen into a routine of going to the hotel, doing all the due diligence together before it opened. She practised cooking, and the same sous chefs he had hired when his business associates had been there worked alongside her in the hotel restaurant, getting familiar with the appliances. They cooked together for the team in place at the hotel for when it opened and, lately, for some VIP families on the island.

While she did her thing, he did his, working remotely from the conference room at the hotel, on call for anyone who might require his input. So it was a little bit puzzling that he was in her company for so much of the time and yet still got a kick from looking at her. He was still so horny for her that he couldn't get enough of her. She could have been wearing sackcloth and ashes with a side order of hobnail boots and he would still have wanted her.

She had set a wonderful table on the veranda. They would be dining al fresco, she'd told him, and it was going to be a very special meal because he had yet to see what she'd been getting up to in the kitchen. All the stuff she'd made so far had been relatively casual and light.

He looked round as he heard her approach from behind. Rafael stared. The light from the conservatory behind illuminated her. She had dressed for the occasion in a frothy lilac dress that he hadn't seen before that skirted her slender thighs and was belted at the waist with a thin, golden cord, and wore flat, strappy sandals and a little necklace with a shell that he had bought for her on impulse at a market they had gone to a few days ago.

She looked like a figure from Greek mythology—a very sexy one.

He slowly walked towards her, smiling as he neared her. 'I like the outfit.'

'Thank you. I got it yesterday at that shop—the one by the boutique that sells those paintings.'

'I didn't see you escape to do that.'

'Because you were working at the hotel and I went to get some stuff from the supermarket. I thought…'

'That you would try and distract me from eating whatever delicacies you've prepared because all I'd be thinking is how much I wanted to eat *you*?'

'That's a very corny line, Rafael.'

But Sammy was smiling as he drew her against him, one hand behind her neck, the other curved possessively over her bottom. Her body curved against him in a way that was exciting and familiar at the same time. She felt the tell-tale dampness spread between her thighs and the sensitivity of her breasts brushing against the silky material. She wasn't wearing a bra; she'd stopped that ages ago. He'd told her that he liked to be able to touch her, lift her top as she walked past in the villa, suckle against her nipple and enjoy her without the faff of having to unclasp bra straps. Since she liked that situation as much as he did, she'd been more than happy to comply.

'I know,' he agreed, grinning. 'I'll try and think of a few better ones. I like the table. You know, there was no need—nothing wrong with us eating in the kitchen.'

'You need to see my talents as a chef!' Sammy smiled. 'Now, if you sit, I'm going to bring our starters out and also the wine.'

'Yes, ma'am.' He was grinning. 'I never knew how much I would enjoy taking orders until you came along.'

Sammy smiled and held back as he strolled towards the table and sat, eyes still on her, hungry and hot. She was surprised and relieved that he hadn't asked her what this special meal was all about. She'd glibly told him that she just wanted to prove her skills, which was true enough, although only part of the story.

Truth was that time was flying by. One week was turning into two. They'd set a time limit but it had been a vague one—two weeks or thereabouts. *Thereabouts*, however, didn't stretch into 'for ever' land. *Thereabouts* meant that they would probably have roughly another week left before he started making noises about returning to the fast lane in London.

When Sammy thought about that, her blood ran cold. Should she wait until he said something—maybe told her that they needed to talk? Was there any way she could brace herself for that kind of conversation? What would she say? Would she just nod, shrug, laugh a bit and then say something vague about it being good while it had lasted?

If she were true to herself, then would that be her response? She had spent the past ten days making sure to hide her growing feelings from Rafael, needing to think things through without him suspecting anything. But now, with their timeline drawing to a close, thinking things through had to come to an end. She would have to take the bull by the horns, do what she had to do and then stand back and see where the cards fell.

She'd chosen the wine, and he rose to relieve her of it as she headed to the table, doing a balancing act with the wine cooler and two bowls of prawns in a spicy pepper sauce. The prawns on the island were the size of lobsters, and just as delicious.

'So, chef, will you tell me about this dish?'

'Try it and you can tell me what you think is in it. It's a game I sometimes play with some of the families I've cooked for in the past. Occasionally service is formal, but a lot of the time I've cooked for stressed out working couples and served up in the kitchens. 'Course, the kitchens aren't quite the sort of kitchens most people are used to—they're kitchens fit for kings and queens.'

'You like that—cooking privately as opposed to in a restaurant?'

'It's a lot more personal, but there's also a lot more resting on what you produce, and sometimes people can be quite difficult. If they're paying, they think they own you.'

'It's like that in any job,' Rafael mused quietly. 'You

get paid to do a service and the person paying is always aware of that. You're working for them and they own you. I saw that with my dad. When we moved to Yorkshire, he got a job, but he was still pretty fragile. There were days when he could barely make it out of bed, but he forced himself, because he knew that he was on a payroll and the minute he stopped doing as he was told the pay would stop.'

'Whenever you talk about your dad, your tone of voice changes.'

'Does it?'

'Hardens.'

Rafael thoughtfully tilted his head to one side. 'I guess it does.' He sighed. 'Not that I talk about this at all, but yes. Growing up, it was hard not to pity my father. Survival and resilience deserted him and the worst of it was that the marriage, as I think I've told you, wasn't a good one. It definitely wasn't made in heaven. But…'

'But? No, wait—don't say a thing. Give me your plate and I'll see to the main meal. I think you're going to love it. It's a very special dish.'

'Need a hand?'

'I've got this.'

Her heart was beating like a sledgehammer as she prepared their mains. She made sure that every garnish was in place and every bit of food on the plate was positioned just so, from the fondant potatoes to the exquisite lobster and the tiny carrots and fresh peas.

He was confiding in her. Was he even aware of that? She didn't think so. She'd barely been aware of it herself until she'd woken up to her own feelings and had begun to take note of the things that were said between them, the little intimacies spoken in passing.

He shared things with her: titbits about his past. He laughed and told her funny stuff that had happened with clients over the years. A couple of days ago, he'd told her of the effort he'd put in to make sure he succeeded because success was everything.

She lapped up those confidences, lashes lowered, hardly breathing, never daring to encourage in case he backed off and turned away.

'Ta-da!' She laughed and flamboyantly laid his plate in front of him. He laughed back and looked at her admiringly.

'A picture should be taken.'

'Already did that.' Sammy slipped into her seat and glanced at him across the flickering candles. 'Can't have a website without lots of images, and I'm doing a lot of work on my website while I'm here. You were saying… about your dad and the way he was after your mother left…?'

'So I was,' Rafael continued absently. 'I was saying that it's partly thanks to you that I've squared off some of my disillusionment with my dad—a hangover from the way I felt all those years ago.'

'How so?'

'You had a rough ride as well and yet you haven't become bitter or cynical. You still believe in love, and you still believe that Mr Right is out there, waiting like a knight in shining armour to marry you and give you the happy-ever-after life you want. You could say I've softened my stance on my father and his life choices. I always loved him but I can see how he could end up a broken guy.'

'I'm really pleased about that although, you know, it's not *quite* as straightforward as Mr Right galloping on his horse towards me.'

'You're not kidding.'

'Although, it's not as impossible as you've come to think.' She felt a fine film of perspiration break out as she wondered where to go from here. Somewhere in the course of the past few days, as she'd untangled her feelings about this man, she'd realised that telling him the truth was going to be the best thing for her. The best way to be her own authentic self.

And she even dared to hope that it would not be in vain. They'd shared a lot. He'd talked to her in a way that she knew, in her gut, he'd never talked to another woman before. He'd told her stuff and, because he wasn't a guy who shared, she'd known that that *stuff* represented true confidences.

He hadn't even been aware of those moments. Like just then, when he'd spoken about his father. Could he see that behind those words lay a world of hurt that he was exposing for her to see? Surely that meant *something*? Sammy knew that he was right when he'd said that, despite what she'd gone through, she still held on to her optimism. She still believed in love. Was she being an idiot to think that he might love her without realising it? That she could tell him how she felt and that he might think about it and realise that he felt the same way? That his heart had been ambushed without him realising, just as hers had?

'What are you thinking?' Rafael looked at the distant expression on Sammy's face. 'That was stupendous, by the way.'

'I know.' She grinned. 'I'm not a bad chef. Maybe one day I'll have a Michelin star.'

'Don't do that. Michelin-starred restaurants can be very overrated, especially for a man who grew up on the wrong side of the tracks.'

'I'll bear that in mind.'

'I was going to ask you what's for dessert, but I've just decided that *you're* going to be my dessert. Come sit on my lap. I want to make love to you right here, right now. Then we can go swim in the pool to cool off. And when we go upstairs we can do it all again.'

'Is sex all you think about, Rafael Moreno?' Sammy laughed but she shuffled off her chair and he adjusted his so that she could straddle him. She linked her fingers behind his head, kissed him slowly and tenderly and then sighed with pleasure when he undid the corded belt from her waist and chucked it on the ground.

She shifted this way and that as he raised the dress, pushing it up to her neck where it gathered in soft folds so that he could lick her swollen nipples. She moaned when he pulled away, looked at them and murmured how beautiful her breasts were.

'Small and perfectly formed,' he observed. 'Touch me, Sammy.'

She laughed huskily and, when she stood up to yank the dress off, followed by her underwear, he did the same with his trousers and tee-shirt until they were both naked and feverish with the excitement that had exploded from nowhere.

He kissed her, pressing her against him. She felt his hardness against her and nearly swooned. Love, passion and desire all merged into something that was overwhelming. She gently pushed him so that he was back in the chair. Then she knelt between his legs and took him into her mouth, touching his thighs and his rigid shaft the way she knew he loved.

His groans of pleasure were such a turn-on, it was an effort to remain there when all she wanted was to straddle him and feel him deep inside her. She raised her eyes to see him arched back in the chair, his big body swamping it, his eyes closed, and she nimbly mounted him and felt the soft, silky slide of his bigness in her with a powerful surge of satisfaction.

She moved on him, slowly then a little faster, and then, as she felt their bodies reaching the same point of no return, she flung her arms around his neck and buried her head against his shoulders as the wonder of her orgasm swept her away.

She was as weak as a kitten when finally the pleasure subsided, and she opened her eyes and sat back, still feeling him in her.

'Rafael,' she murmured huskily.

'Jesus, that was amazing.'

'You mean that?'

'Of course I do.' He smiled. 'The ground moves every time…incredible. If I were ever to be caught up in an actual earthquake, no one would be able to say that I wouldn't know what it felt like.'

'It's the same for me.'

'Glad to hear it.' He stroked his fingers through her hair and their eyes tangled in a lengthening silence. Sammy could feel the pulse in her temple beating steadily as she continued to look at him and this time there was no hiding what she was feeling. She'd spent enough time covering up her feelings for this guy. Now was the time for truth or else they would part company and the moment would be lost.

'Sammy…'

'You know what I want to say, don't you?' she murmured gruffly.

'No, I don't. Don't say it, Sammy.'

'I'm in love with you, Rafael.'

'You're not.'

He fidgeted and she eased off him to stand back, valiantly looking at him, proud of her nudity and wanting him to see the woman who wanted to live her life uninhibited with the man she loved.

He didn't meet her eyes and she swallowed and slowly put the dress back on. Her body was still hot and sticky from love-making, although somewhere inside her something was shutting down. But she wasn't going to give this up without a fight.

'Don't tell me what I am, Rafael.'

'This wasn't part of the plan.'

'Plans don't always work out the way you think they're going to. I didn't even like you when I first met you, and I fooled myself for ages that you weren't the sort of guy for me, even though I was attracted to you.'

'I need to get dressed.'

Sammy looked away, for the first time feeling the space between them and holding on to her pride with difficulty, but determined to speak her mind and to heck with it.

When she next looked at him, they were no longer lovers but uncertain strangers staring across a divide. At least that was what it felt like to her. She saw the way he had shut down. His expression was shuttered and defensive.

'Rafael, I know how you feel about love and commitment and marriage and all that stuff…'

'I honestly don't know where you're going with this, and it's not something I want to talk about.'

'You're afraid of involvement and afraid of being open to your emotions. But look at us for the past few weeks, Rafael: we've been brilliant together. We've shared things, we've talked…and I mean *really* talked. You don't want to admit it but you're like me. I didn't want to fall in love with you because you didn't make any sense for me and my life, but I did. Sometimes you just can't help what happens to your heart. Maybe it was the same for you.'

Sammy looked at him hopelessly. She breathed in deeply but already her mind was running ahead, predicting the inevitable outcome. She would have to leave.

She was speaking her mind and everything she was saying was falling on barren ground because the signs hadn't been there—not for him. It really had just been a physical attraction for him and, even if it hadn't, even if he felt something for her, his beliefs were too ingrained for him ever to change them.

Mentally, she was packing her suitcase. The soft sounds of insects, the warm, still tropical air, the darkness of the pool and the optimistically laid out table now seemed horribly mocking, so she tried not to look at any of it but to keep her eyes firmly focused on the man gazing at her with cool, unreadable eyes.

'I'm sorry to disappoint you, Sammy, but no. It wasn't the same for me. I am not a man who's in search of love. I never have been and I never will be. I thought we were on the same page. If I'd had the slightest idea that you might begin thinking that this charade we've been playing was the real thing, then there's no way I would ever have involved you in it in the first place.'

'No,' she agreed dully.

'I like you, Sammy.' His voice gentled. 'But liking isn't loving. Liking is enjoying someone's company.'

'Okay.' She looked up at him. He was being kind and she couldn't stand it. 'I think I'm going to pack and get back home.'

'I think that's a good idea. I can arrange a flight back for you tomorrow.'

'Sure. Thank you.'

'In the meantime, I'll go to the hotel. Everything's

ready for the opening in a month's time. There's no harm in sampling the product.'

'Quite.'

'And Sammy…?'

She was beginning to turn away. She twisted to look at him over her shoulder, one last glance at the guy who had turned her world upside down.

'Yes?'

'I'm sorry I couldn't give you what you wanted. But, trust me, one day you'll look back at what we had and you'll thank me, because you'll know that I would never have been good for you. You deserve the guy who meets your checklist.'

She nodded and turned away.

Rafael felt as though time had suddenly slowed down. His brain was sluggishly receiving information but processing it was painful—painful but necessary.

He watched as she walked away from him into the house without bothering to slide the glass doors shut behind her. For a while he was frozen, staring at nothing in particular, then he moved to one of the chairs by the pool and sat staring at the glassy water.

He should have known. He should have read the signs. She was romantic. She believed in love and she wanted the happy-ever-after. The second they had embarked on their charade, he should have known that there was a chance that sooner or later what was false had a chance of merging into something real.

For her. For him, it was all just the physical stuff.

Okay, so they'd talked, they got along. But he was standing firm by what he'd said, that *getting along* wasn't the same as *falling in love* and surrendering his soul into the safekeeping of someone else. There was no leap of faith involved in *getting along* with someone.

This hadn't been about drifting into coupledom for him. He had vivid memories of the amount of time his father had wasted on love. He had drowned trying to resuscitate it when it was well and truly dead, and where had that got him? Rafael had been left picking up too many pieces not to have learnt valuable lessons from the experience. Lessons that had protected him from the very thing that had happened to Sammy!

He had sworn never to put himself in a position of vulnerability, open to hurt and pain, and in a place where others might suffer because of his choices. She would be better off without him. She was a special person who needed to find her soul mate.

Uneasy with his introspection, Rafael glanced up at the bank of bedroom windows. He couldn't see her, because the shutters were closed, but he knew that she would be packing. He texted his PA and told her immediately to book a flight out of the country for Sammy and that her details would be on file. It was done. Half an hour later, his phone pinged with the message that the relevant information had been sent to Sammy.

Making up his mind, Rafael stood up and headed indoors, already on his phone telling the guys at the hotel that he would be testing the sleeping quarters for the next couple of nights.

'Make sure the mattresses are comfortable,' he said, heading to his office to complete the call and gather up the work-related stuff which he would do once he was at the hotel. 'We don't want any guests deciding that they're too hard, too soft, too lumpy or just not up to scratch. Wealthy guests always expect the best.' As an afterthought, he phoned through to the hotel again and asked for a team to be sent to clean the villa as soon as possible.

He knew Sammy. He knew that she would be packing and probably apprehensive about bumping into him.

He scowled as it struck him that he was reluctant to bump into her as well. Everything that had just happened in the past half hour should have turned him off big time but when he thought of her, as he was thinking of her now, his body reacted in unpredictable ways.

He still wanted her. Still craved her.

He would wait an hour then he would go pack a bag and head to the hotel. She would be gone the following morning and…life would return to normal. He might have shared more with Sammy than he had with any other woman but, in the end, he was insulated against the very thing she had wanted. She would ease out of his life just like every other woman had, barely leaving a ripple behind her.

CHAPTER TEN

RAFAEL KNEW JUST when Sammy left the island.

In fact, he was in the hotel when he heard the sound of the aeroplane that would deliver her back to England; that was how small the island was. It had roared overhead, and he'd gritted his teeth and tried not to think of her staring out of the window, her heart hardening in the face of his rejection.

Within the week, he too would return to England, and henceforth business dealings with her would be done via his PA. There was no need for him to know anything about what she did with the considerable amount of money he would be handing over to her.

And, as for their fake engagement, it might have been whispered to Sammy's mother but it had not ignited in the press, so when he returned, there would be no public curiosity to douse.

As for Caroline Payne, he was sure that Sammy would retreat from the make-believe fantasy with no harm done to her relationship with her mother. She would be the decisive one who had cut the ties, having realised the error of her headlong rush into infatuation. She had poured her heart out to him in a no-holds-barred performance that he could only admire, and she would surely be bitter at the way he had reacted—coolly, firmly, with no way back for discussion.

Of course, she would tell whatever story she wished to tell to her mother, and he couldn't fault that approach. Bitterness would fuel her. He would be in the lead role as Big Bad Wolf, knocked back for the first time in his life, dismissed to lick his wounds in a dark cave somewhere, and he was happy with that. He couldn't be happier.

A woman in love with him? No way. He blamed himself because he had been swept away by the sex. The truth was that love had never been a complication he would take on board—*could* take on board—however convenient the situation was and however hot the sex.

And however warm the laughter, stimulating the conversation, tender the touches...

He closed his eyes and breathed heavily. She'd left yesterday and it felt like a lifetime ago.

The conference room at the hotel should have been his sanctuary. Work had always been his go-to, but now, with his laptop in front of him and a string of emails to deal with, he just couldn't focus. His chest hurt. His eyes hurt. His *brain* hurt. In his mind's eye, he saw her thinking, reflecting, remembering. She would remember everything—the way she had walked into love and the way she had proudly told him how she felt, even though it must have been daunting for her, given everything he had said in the past about not believing in love.

Would she already have been to see her mum? Or would she be bracing herself, buying some time before she launched into a smiling, self-deprecating, eye-rolling speech about what an idiot she'd been, and thank God she'd seen the light before it was too late?

And in her heart? In her heart, she would remember the good things they'd had, but in her head, he would crystallise into the sort of guy she knew she should have stayed away from. If she forgot the way she'd confessed her love, then she would never forget the way he'd rejected her.

How fast could love harden, only to be replaced by hate and then eventually indifference? She would look back over her shoulder and curse herself for her foolishness in falling for him.

Rafael surrendered to his thoughts and snapped shut the laptop. Through the bank of windows, he could see the endless stretch of blue sky, and in the distance the streak of turquoise ocean turning dark as it meshed with the horizon. It was not yet four in the afternoon. He felt he could keep sitting right here, staring through the window, until that blue sky turned violet and orange and then finally inky black. The swirl of his thoughts paralysed him. He'd led a nomadic life when it came to the opposite sex. But Sammy...

He pressed his thumbs against his eyes and felt sick. Always able to see problems clearly, Rafael was caught in the unusual place of not knowing what to think or what was really going on. He had a pounding headache.

He poured himself a glass of whisky. It wasn't going to help, but he downed it anyway. He scowled at the empty glass in his hand and all over again succumbed to the second-guessing he'd been trying to keep at bay.

In love with him… She'd told him that he was the last person she could ever fall for. She'd said that she went for a type and he wasn't that type. She had her check-list! Had he been at fault for taking her at her word and believing what she had said? Or had he been so busy enjoying her that he'd steered clear of asking questions to which the answers might have proven unpalatable?

But she was gone, and she would thank him for turning her away; would thank him for putting her back on the path to finding the sort of guy she deserved. He wasn't that guy. He wasn't a guy who did love. How many times had he made that clear? A thousand! Yet she had defiantly ploughed ahead, ignoring what he had told her. She was someone who forged forward. That was just her trademark. She braced herself and fearlessly went where angels feared to tread. He should have taken that into account! Sammy was a law unto herself.

His stomach tightened again and he felt a stab of pain deep inside.

Well, as it stood, whatever love she had would sour quickly…but again that thought twisted something inside him. Looking at the bigger picture, though, it would still be for her own good! He would end up being the fall guy in a big way but that was what he wanted, wasn't it? He'd actively volunteered to be the fall guy.

Rafael paced the room as the evening wore into night, barely seeing anything, aware of the darkness outside getting thicker and denser until the Technicolor tropical landscape outside became shadowy shapes and forms.

Where was she now? He felt haunted by the memory of her face and those green eyes resting on him, seeing deep into him in a way no one else ever had.

He called his PA. He would accelerate his flight back. He needed to leave immediately. There were things to do…no, memories to be contained…and they couldn't be contained here. That done and sorted, Rafael eyed the whisky, reluctantly dismissed the temptation for a top up and instead scooped up his laptop and headed out of the hotel, back to his villa.

Maybe he could leave the thinking behind there. It worked for the length of time it took him to get back to the villa, and only because he had to concentrate on the dark, twisty roads, only sporadically lit, the sort of roads where one small mistake could land his car a little too close to a coconut tree for comfort.

But, the second he was inside his villa—which felt as empty as a wedding venue after all the guests had left and the band had packed up and gone—he sat down in the conservatory and let loose a groan of hurt and despair.

He barely recognised the sound. He leant forward to bury his head in his hands and then, like a swarm of insects released from the safety of a box in which they had been conveniently contained, his thoughts rushed to attack him. He remembered every tender touch, every glance, every smile, every wicked, teasing grin… He could recall how he'd felt when he'd been with her: complete, happy. In no rush to go anywhere, do anything or even think too hard.

She'd reminded him about how they'd talked. He'd responded that *talking* had meant nothing, that it was just a fact that they'd got along, and *getting along* wasn't love.

But he'd done much more than talk to her. He'd opened up. He'd let go of the restraints that had kept him prisoner all his life. He'd confided and shared all those little bits of him he'd become used to keeping to himself and he hadn't even noticed that he'd been doing it.

How could he not have clued in to the obvious? It all added up now: that lazy urge to hold on to what they had; the cold feeling of desperation when he'd thought of her walking away from him; and then, this evening, this sickening horror at a vision of life slipping between his fingers.

Because a life without her in it was no life at all. He'd been so busy polishing the armour he'd spent a lifetime putting in place to protect his heart that he hadn't seen what would have been obvious to an idiot: he'd fallen in love with her.

He couldn't say when or how but he just knew that he had…and now? Now, she'd be busy unravelling what they had built, toughening up and hardening her emotions. She'd be building walls he would never be able to break down, building them with disillusionment and bitterness.

He had to see her. The time between this decision and the flight he had booked, which was just a matter of a handful of hours, felt like a lifetime. If he could have arranged for his private jet to swing by and pick him up like a handy taxi service, he would have, but he still had to pack anyway.

He still had last minute things to do. One of those things was to text her and tell her that he would be coming to see her. He had to know that she would be in, although he would just have gone and waited for as long as it took.

He didn't say why. He simply said that something urgent had come up and that he would have to see her face to face to discuss it. He'd said he would meet her at her house, or she could come to his office—anywhere that suited.

So he was meeting her at his office, and her reply suggested that as far as she was concerned the office was the place for a business discussion. Reading between the lines of her cool, brief response, he got the impression that she had already shut the doors on him and that only the hint that it might be work-oriented had motivated her to agree to see him.

He'd take that.

He couldn't relax. The adrenaline was surging through him and it only began to abate when the plane touched down the following day. He'd asked if she could swing by his office at five-thirty. There would still be people around, of course, but that was okay, because he didn't want her to feel nervous, to feel that there would be just the two of them. If she now hated him, then the last thing he wanted was for her to see an empty office, turn skittish and run away, work talk or no work talk.

* * *

Sammy was dabbing her eyes when her mobile pinged and she stared down at Rafael's name on her phone. She'd barely been back in the country and the last person she'd expected to hear from was him. He'd rejected her. She'd said what she had to say, but there hadn't even been a second when he'd considered what she'd told him, not a second when he'd given any thought to the possibility that he might have feelings for her. He'd been appalled. *Love her?* How could she have been foolish enough to think that he might have fallen for her like she'd fallen for him?

The speed of his rejection had said it all.

She'd packed, knowing that he was sitting outside on that veranda with the remains of her specially prepared meal scattered on the table, cruelly lit with the romantic glow of the candles she had taken time to buy and put there. They hadn't even got round to the chocolate fondant she had made.

When had he disappeared off to the hotel? She didn't know, because she'd made sure to stick to her room and pack, only emerging when she knew for certain that he would no longer be in the house. She hadn't cried. The tears had lodged inside her, refusing to come out. They hadn't been able to get past the pain—the pain of her rejected love and the agony of the emptiness that lay ahead, which she would have to fill somehow.

On the flight over, she'd wondered whether she should go to Yorkshire and see her mum immediately so that she could get the whole sorry situation off her chest. She wasn't quite sure what she intended to say but she knew that she would just say whatever it took to make sure her mother didn't get into too much of a state. That would mean plastering a phony, confident smile on her face and launching into some spiel about finding out in the nick of time that she and Rafael weren't suited.

Since she hadn't been able to face the phony smile just yet, she had decided to go to London and stay there for a few days. She knew people there. One of the girls who had come through culinary college with her had her own small flat in Notting Hill, so Sammy had arranged to stay with her for a few days.

'I'll cook,' she'd promised, 'and clean up behind me. I know that's the bit you always hated!'

So, when she'd got Rafael's text, she'd felt the breath leave her in a whoosh. She'd just come back from a very speedy supermarket shop and had been about to sit down, relax and deal with her jet lag.

He wanted to see her. It would be about business, of course, and she'd been tempted to tell him just to email whatever he wanted to say, but then she'd thought that a series of emails between them would only prolong the misery and keep him alive in her head. Whereas, if she went to see him, spent fifteen minutes hearing whatever he had to say, it would be like lancing a boil—over and done with, only the healing left to endure.

And besides, a little voice had piped up, *you know you want to see him...want to have one last look at that beautiful face and put it in your memory bank so that you can pull it out to gaze at at a later date.*

She had squashed that little voice. She wasn't going to succumb to thinking about him twenty-four-seven even, though she knew that that was exactly what she would probably end up doing. She told herself that, when she saw him, she would make sure to remember the way he had rejected her. She decided that seeing him would give her the sense of closure that she hadn't had when she'd left him out there on the veranda with the warm, tropical breeze and the harmonious sounds of insects, frogs and toads reminding her that there really was no such thing as paradise.

He'd suggested going to Yorkshire but the last thing she wanted was for him to meet her anywhere private. The thought of him in her house had been way too much. That would have left her way too vulnerable. They could meet in his office, surrounded by phones, desks, computers and people working hard making money, and that would be fine.

Still, as she got dressed the following day with a sickening sensation of *déjà vu* in the pit of her stomach, she almost wished that she'd gone for the response for him to email anything he had to say because, whatever he said, there was nothing that couldn't be communicated in writing. Was there?

Rafael could feel the tension building as the time approached to meet her.

Part of him wondered whether she might bail at the last minute, in which case he wasn't entirely sure what he would do. He could hardly pursue her if she really didn't want to lay eyes on him.

Then he wasted some time wondering whether he should meet her in the foyer of the building. Finally, he decided against that because, if the only reason she had agreed to meet him at all was that she thought it was to do with work, then being shown up by one of the receptionists would confirm that. He had tactfully dispatched his PA.

Rafael was a man who was impervious to nerves. Something about having spent his life beating the odds had strengthened his inner core, made him utterly resilient when it came to facing down challenges and making the best of whatever life decided to throw at him.

But right now, drumming his fingers on his desk and resisting the urge to prowl through his office to relieve his tension, he was nervous. He felt vulnerable and hesitant, and for some reason that had made him think of his dad, had made him re-evaluate the black and white vision he had had of him as a man who had lacked the strength to give up on the unattainable.

His father had simply been human, and being human was the very thing Rafael had spent his life trying hard not to be. To be human was to be weak, and being weak was something he had made sure he would never be.

But he was here and he felt *human* for the first time. He hadn't stopped beating himself up for his stubborn blindness in recognising what had been staring him in the face. And yet, how was he to have known that, just when he wasn't expecting it, someone would break down all the barriers he had constructed around himself? His wealth, power and status had made him invincible and, in his head, his iron will had cemented his own formidable belief that the only person who could ever control the direction of his life would be himself. How wrong he'd been.

He stilled when the call came through that Sammy had arrived. He waited, seated behind his desk, counting the seconds until she entered his office. It had only been a matter of hours and yet, as he saw her framed in the door that opened into his PA's office beyond his, Rafael felt as though he was seeing her for the first time.

It felt like being punched in the gut. She was as slight as he remembered, as graceful as a gazelle, and her face was tight and cautious. Her body language screamed discomfort and he rose to his feet and walked towards her.

'Sammy… I wasn't sure whether you would come.'

'You didn't leave me much choice. I'm here because you said you had something to say to me face to face.'

'Yes.'

'Well, go ahead and say it.'

'Come through to my office, please. I can't…say what I want to say with you standing with your back to the door.'

She'd dressed in a prim navy skirt, some workmanlike shoes and a white jumper with a thick jacket swamping her. It made him think of her in those sexy summer outfits she had worn, braless and so sexy that she'd always managed to blow his self-control straight out of the water.

He raked his fingers through his hair, shifting uncomfortably, and looked down at his shoes, feeling a bit like a school kid summoned to the principal's office to discuss being caught smoking behind the bike shed. Although, in fairness, he'd faced many a hauling into the principal's office and had never felt like this in any of them.

'I don't intend to stay long, Rafael. Say what you have to say. If I need to sign anything, then I'll do that and leave.'

'Nothing to sign.' He walked back into his office and breathed a sigh of relief when she followed him through to perch on the chair in front of his desk.

'I…' he began. 'I… I see that you got back in one piece.'

'I haven't come here for the chit-chat.'

'I can understand why you're angry with me.'

'I also haven't come here to rake up what's been said between us. That's over and done with and I'm moving on.'

They stared at one another in silence. Lost for words, Rafael cleared his throat and thought that he had seen a million sides of her but never this side—this tough, steely side, closed off and shuttered—not even when she had stormed into his office to see him that very first time.

Just bite the bullet.

'Sammy, I had to see you, had to talk to you. What I have to say could never have been said in an email because I just wouldn't have known how to put it into words. You're here and I've missed you,' he said quietly in an all-or-nothing impulse. 'I've been a fool.'

'What are you trying to say? I don't understand.'

'And I don't blame you because the last conversation we had involved me telling you that there was no way I could… I could…return your feelings.'

'Rafael, I won't sit here and listen to you say stuff that isn't true!'

'I never lie. Haven't I told you that already?'

'You're also a guy who likes to get what he wants. Do you think that you can say things you believe I want to hear to get me back into bed with you?'

'Please, Sammy, hear me out. We got into a game that had consequences and that game was my idea. A quid pro quo situation was how I thought of it at the time, a favour that carried mutual benefits for both of us. And then…then…the game got a lot more serious than either of us had planned.

'It was selfish of me to get you involved with an ex who was hell-bent on revenge. I knew that, if Clement pulled out of the deal, people's livelihoods would be on the line and I put that ahead of any repercussions that might have happened between us. It never crossed my mind that I couldn't handle the charade. I presented it to you as a deal that would pay off and would cost us nothing because that's what I believed.'

'It's fair to say that the blame for that stupid charade falls on both our shoulders,' Sammy muttered gruffly.

'Then what started as a game became serious. We became lovers.' He watched as colour surged into her cheeks and she lowered her eyes. 'And, like an idiot, I continued thinking that I would continue to have complete control over that situation as well. The truth is that

I have *always* had complete control over my emotions…
that is, until you came along.'

Sammy looked up and their eyes met. Her heart leapt inside her because she could see the blinding sincerity on
his face. Hope began to send shoots through her.

'I'm listening,' she said breathlessly.

'I felt sick when I watched you walk through those
patio doors but I was paralysed. I didn't know what to do.
I told myself that the sick feeling would go, told myself
that I could never return your love because I was inca-
pable of feeling love. I didn't know how to handle what
you'd said and I had no other responses in my repertoire.
I fell back on what I thought was the truth when, in fact,
I'd left that truth behind the second you walked into my
life. I denied feelings I never even recognised because
I'd never had them before.'

'And suddenly you changed in a matter of hours?'
Sammy tried to sound incredulous, but it was difficult,
because she knew that he was being honest, even though
she could scarcely believe it.

'I did. When truth caught up with the lies I'd been telling myself. When the thought of not having you in my
life made me want to cry. I love you, Sammy, and, more
than that I need you, because there's no point to my life
without you in it. I just hope I'm not too late to have you
accept my offer of marriage. Not for show, just for us—
me and you for ever.'

Their eyes met and tangled, just as they had many
times in the past, but this time what Sammy saw was

the heart she'd yearned for in those dark eyes; a heart this beautiful, strong, proud man was handing to her for safekeeping.

She smiled, slowly at first, and then radiantly and widely, because her own heart was bursting with love.

'Yes,' she murmured, tiptoeing to kiss the side of his mouth and then brushing her finger where her lips had lingered. 'Yes, I think marrying you is just the thing I want to do. This is going to be our fairy tale, Rafael Moreno. And, trust me, it's a fairy tale that's never going to end.'

* * * * *

Did you fall in love with
Emergency Engagement?

Then why not try these other fabulous stories
by Cathy Williams!

The Italian's Innocent Cinderella
Unveiled as the Italian's Bride
Bound by Her Baby Revelation
A Wedding Negotiation with Her Boss
Royally Promoted

Available now!